A Cowboy and His Skipped Christmas

Sweet Contemporary Cowboy Romance,
Chestnut Ranch Romance, Book 8

Emmy Eugene

ISBN-13: 979-8663992169

CHAPTER 1

Theo Lange swung down from the huge chestnut bay he rode, reaching for his gloves in the next moment. Life certainly wasn't dull at The Singer Ranch, but Theo could use an afternoon where he didn't sweat through his clothes as he literally chased errant cattle.

"Ho, there," he called, stepping up onto the bottom rung of the fence. He waved one arm above his head to the two or three cowboys in the field.

A couple of dogs barked, and that got everyone to turn and look at Theo. He balanced and waved both hands above his head in the sign he'd learned to indicate they had livestock on the loose.

The three men swung toward him, one of them—probably Jake—whistling at the cattle canines they used. The blue heelers streaked toward Theo, and he did absolutely love them.

He didn't love much else about this operation. Robert

Singer was a tough, old man, and he did not mince words. Theo had witnessed him dress down one of the best cowboys on the ranch, then lay into the foreman, and then press one hand against his son's chest when Ben had tried to intervene.

Theo had stood there in complete shock, wishing he could make himself smaller just in case Robert's attention somehow zeroed in on him. When the old cowboy had turned toward the line of guys, Theo had dropped his eyes to the ground and hid his face with the wide brim on his cowboy hat.

He got back in the saddle on a horse he'd named Bear, because all horses should have names. He'd learned that none of the horses here had names, and that was just unacceptable to Theo.

The dogs had names, and they seemed open to the constant stream of people moving on and off the ranch. Theo had made better friends with them than anyone else on the ranch in the last two months since he'd been here.

"They've broken through that temporary fence on Road Twelve," he said as the other cowboys joined him. The dogs streaked ahead of them, and Theo moved his horse into a trot to follow the others.

He wasn't as good with a rope as they were, because he didn't spend his days in a saddle, throwing ropes, and herding cattle back where they belonged. He missed Fox Hollow with a fierceness he'd thought he'd been ready for.

He had not been ready. He had never in a million years thought he'd be this miserable. He slept on the bottom bunk in a shared bedroom, with two more cowboys across the hall. The four of them shared a tiny bathroom, and Theo barely had time to grab a few swallows of coffee before he left the cabin bright and early.

Since he was the last one who'd come to The Singer Ranch in his cabin, he was the low man on the totem pole. He showered last. He got the dregs of the coffee. The ends of the bread.

As he rode behind the others, Theo wondered how his life had come to this moment.

You don't need this job, he thought. He didn't need the job, and his desire to quit pulled through him with utmost strength.

He did not want to be here anymore.

His bank account had plenty of money in it, and he wanted his own house. He could get a couple of his own horses, name them what he wanted, and get a pair of dogs to go with them.

He'd thought he wanted to hide, and he'd never been much for displaying how much money he had. At this point, he'd take a one-bedroom cabin where he got up and made his own coffee and then scrambled his own eggs.

He veered to the left to head off the cattle making a turn that way. His thoughts would not be distracted though, and he couldn't believe how good his life had been at Fox Hollow.

An image of Sorrell Adams filled his mind, blocking out the black beef cows trying to make his life difficult. He yipped at them, and Bluebell barked at the cattle, sending them back toward Roland, Jake, and Sam.

By the time they got the cattle contained, Theo had made up his mind.

He was done at The Singer Ranch. At this point, he'd leave behind everything he'd brought with him. He just wanted to get in his truck and go to the first hotel he could find.

That wasn't entirely true. He wanted to go to the first hotel he could find that had an on-site restaurant, room service, and air conditioning.

He brushed down his horse, finished his chores, and walked over to the administration building. It was one of the newer buildings on the ranch, and a blast of cool air hit him in the face when he entered.

Thanksgiving would arrive next week, but Texas hadn't seemed to have gotten the memo yet, and the sun still super-heated everything under its broad face.

"Hey, Courtney," Theo said, tipping his hat to the woman. "Is Winn at his desk?"

"He just went over to the barn office."

Theo pivoted, determined to talk to Winn today. The thought of waking up in the morning and working through another twelve hours, with people he didn't know, and no connection to anyone or anything had his chest tightening immensely.

He left his truck in front of the administration building and strode toward the barn. He went in the side door and turned into the office, relief flooding him when he saw Winn standing at his desk.

He glanced up from the computer. "Hey, Theo," Winn said.

"Hey." Theo took a deep breath. "Listen, I know this could cause a problem for you, but I just can't do this anymore."

Winn stopped typing on the keyboard and looked up fully. "I thought you were a career cowboy."

Theo pressed his teeth together and reminded himself that yes, that was the persona he'd put forward for the past several years. "I just need a change," he said. "I thought a new ranch would do it, but I was wrong."

He hated the work here, and his fingers twitched to be on his way.

"All right," Winn said. "I hate to lose you. You're one of the hardest workers we've had."

"I appreciate that," Theo said. "I'm really sorry."

"It's okay," Winn said. He reached for something in the desk. He'd built it himself, and Theo liked the standing desk, which had a sloped top to hold Ben's computer, and a few drawers down the front of it.

He took out a paper and handed it to Theo. Their eyes met, and Theo could almost see a mirror of his dark eyes in the brown depth's of Ben's.

He worked all the time, despite being married with children. Theo had never seen him in anything but a pair of jeans, cowboy boots, a button-down shirt in a variety of patterns and colors, and that cream-colored cowboy hat.

Theo wished he wanted to be as predictable. He hated routine, though, and as he stood there and listened to Winn talk about the paper he wanted Theo to sign to terminate his employment at The Singer Ranch, Theo started planning his vacation.

"Where are you going to go now?" Winn asked, handing the pen to Theo.

He signed his name, and said, "I don't know." He glanced up at the man who had hired him. "I'll just get my next paycheck via direct deposit?"

"Sure thing," Winn said, already back to his computer.

Theo's phone beeped at him, and he really wanted to see what that notification was from his Dow Jones app. He only had specific ones set, and it must be an important one.

"Thanks," Theo said, and he ducked out of the barn office. He checked his phone, and the price of Continental had reached the high he'd set.

He didn't even have time to walk back to his truck. He moved fast, because the clock was ticking in New York. Six minutes until the Dow closed, and Theo needed to get rid of Continental right now.

In the morning, everyone would be trying to unload, and the stock price would fall. He'd learned from his father to be ruthless when it came to selling. He couldn't hold onto stocks because he hoped they'd do something.

They're predictable, Theodore, his dad used to say. *Buy low. Sell high. Set a limit, and when it's reached, sell. Don't wait.*

Don't hesitate.

Theo didn't hesitate, and he quickly tapped a few times, finally touching the green SELL button and confirming it.

Three minutes to spare, and the six thousand shares of Continental left his account. He sighed as he leaned against the wall, then he got himself out of the barn and back to the microscopic cabin where he'd been living for the last couple of months.

He'd shown up with a couple of suitcases, and he left with the same, his roommates just watching him. "You're leaving?" Martin asked.

"Yes," Theo said, putting a smile on his face. Standing there, he realized how unhappy he was.

"Going somewhere else?" Kent asked.

"Not another ranch, no," Theo said. He quickly ran through his list of belongings, telling himself he could literally buy anything he left behind. A new toothbrush, a pair of boots, a set of plates. None of it mattered.

"It's been great," he lied, keeping his smile hitched in place. The others responded likewise, and Theo made his exit from The Singer Ranch without fanfare.

As he drove away, the heavy relief filling him did buoy his mood.

He hated this time of year, and he really just wanted to skip the holidays completely. His father had died the day before Christmas, and Theo did his best to participate in as few holiday events as possible.

This year, without anywhere to belong, he could skip Christmas completely.

The idea appealed to him like nothing else had, and with

the sale of his Continental stock, he'd just made almost a million dollars.

He could skip anything he wanted.

He drove to Austin and pulled over to search for the nicest hotel he could find. Then he went down a couple of steps and navigated to a three-and-a-half star hotel that had a pool, suites, the restaurant he wanted, and bonus—a park right across the street.

Theo's gratitude doubled when he asked for a suite and they had one. He showered in hot water for the first time in months, sighing as he did.

He put on gym shorts and a T-shirt, left his cowboy hat in his suite, and headed down to the restaurant. He needed a steak to celebrate his freedom from The Singer Ranch, and that would give him enough energy to check his stocks, plan a day at the park tomorrow, and then figure out where he should go so he could leave Christmas behind this year.

Downstairs, he stepped to the podium, the lights inside the restaurant dim and the music low. "Do I need a reservation?" he asked.

"No, sir," the woman drawled, glancing up. "Are you a guest here?" She wore a pretty smile, and Theo finally felt like he had enough energy and reason to return it.

"Yes." His pulse did nothing when looking at this woman, though he supposed she was attractive. The problem was, his heart had been beating for Sorrell Adams—and only Sorrell Adams—for so long, he wasn't even sure if he'd recognize attraction to another woman.

"Do you want me to put the charges on your room?" she asked.

"Sure." He gave her his room number, and she turned to take him to a table. He'd taken one step when a woman to his left and behind him said, "Theo?"

He knew who he'd see even as he turned his head toward the woman that had been torturing him since the day he started at Fox Hollow Ranch.

"Sorrell," he said, drinking her in. She'd curled that gorgeous hair so it fell in loose waves over her shoulders. She wore makeup so well that it enhanced her natural beauty, and she looked like she'd just come from a meeting.

He noticed that she stood with someone, and Theo looked to him.

His chest tightened again, and he didn't want to hear her introduce him to her new boyfriend. She'd refused him so many times, and he could not stand the thought of her going out with someone else.

"Good to see you," he said, his voice tight. He turned to follow the hostess, ramming right into the podium. Pain shot through his ribs and down into his stomach, and he couldn't stop the grunt as it flew from his mouth.

Humiliation flowed through him now, and he shot a glance at Sorrell, who still stood there with her new cowboy boyfriend, and Theo dodged the podium and walked away as fast as he could.

CHAPTER 2

Sorrell Adams stared after the only man she wanted to talk to. The only man she wanted to be with.

Her heart hammered in her chest, and every cell in her body seemed to be vibrating. She pulled in breath after breath, her mind racing as she tried to figure out what to do.

"You better go after him," Lance said.

"Should I?" Sorrell asked, looking at her secretary. She hated this weakness in her, but her eyes had already started to fill with tears.

The last two months had been some of the hardest of her life, and she honestly thought she'd never see Theo Lange again.

Why was he here?

Was God trying to play some trick on her? She hadn't been to Austin in years, and the one time she was here for training on a new software system, she ran into Theo Lange?

She pressed one hand to her heart, still at a complete loss as to what to do.

"Let's go," Lance said, actually taking her hand and towing her toward the podium. The woman that Theo had been talking to returned to the podium, and she glanced at them.

"Two?"

"Actually, no," Lance said, and Sorrell was glad he was taking charge. She felt like a fool, but right now, she needed him. That was their professional relationship. She helped him sometimes, and sometimes he assisted her.

She'd never shared much of her personal life with him, but Lance had eyes, and he'd obviously seen something between Sorrell and Theo.

"She just needs to sit with that man you just took back." Lance leaned into the podium and put a dashing smile on his face. "And I need to know what time you get off."

"Oh, my word," Sorrell said, staring at him now. How could he say things like that? She couldn't even imagine having that kind of confidence.

The woman giggled and said, "I'm not off until midnight, sir." She glanced at Sorrell. "And he's in a booth, so there's room for you."

Sorrell could never walk through the restaurant and slide into the booth across from Theo.

"I'll take her back," Lance said, still smiling for all he was worth. He knocked a couple of times on the podium, seized her hand again, and took her with him.

"No," she said, trying to dig in her heels, but the floor in this place was smooth and shiny. "I can't."

"You can," Lance said, easily towing her along. "And you will."

"You don't even know who he is," Sorrell said.

"Sure I do," Lance said. "He's Theo, and he's the one you think about when I catch you staring at nothing in your office."

Sorrell didn't even know she'd been doing that. She had been quite unfocused at work since Theo's departure from the ranch, because she'd lost her whole support system when he'd left her life.

"Sir," Lance said, pouring Southern charm into his tone now. "We overbooked, and this lovely lady needs a seat. You have one, so we're going to put her right here with you."

Sorrell met Theo's gaze, and though she could hardly see in only the low light stuck to the wall on the inside of the booth, she definitely saw something flash in Theo's eyes.

She wasn't sure if it was anger or desire. He could easily look around and see this restaurant was practically empty, but he nodded to the other side of the table. "She took the other menu."

"Oh, Sorrell doesn't eat a whole lot," Lance said easily. He almost shoved Sorrell into the booth. "Our meetings don't start until ten, but that doesn't mean you can stay out too late tonight." He flicked his gaze to Theo. "Boss."

With that, Lance walked away, and Sorrell swore she heard him chuckle to himself.

She sat in the booth, quivering in front of the one

person she'd always been the most comfortable with, and she hated that.

When he'd left, she'd lost so much.

Tell him, she thought.

Seren had been telling her to just text Theo and tell him how she felt. Her sister wanted Sorrell to ask Theo out, but Sorrell didn't know how to do that. She didn't understand the order the words needed to be in.

"What are you doing here?" he asked, his focus completely on the menu.

"New software training," she said.

"How long will you be here?"

"Through Sunday." Sorrell had nothing to look at and nothing to occupy her hands. She could look at Theo's handsome face all day and all night, and right now, she was staring at him.

He hadn't been shaving at his new ranch, and Sorrell rather liked the full beard and mustache. He wasn't wearing a cowboy hat tonight, and he looked so...normal.

"What about you?" she asked, hating the formalities between them.

"I'm undecided," he said.

"Undecided?"

He finally looked up and passed her the menu, his eyes skating all over the place. "Yes. Undecided."

"What does that mean?"

"I think you'll like the egg roll appetizers," he said, and Sorrell felt like they were having four different conversations.

She wouldn't be able to eat much at all, not with the way her stomach was currently shrieking at her.

"Something to drink?" the waiter asked. "You don't have a menu."

"It's fine," Theo said. "I've looked, and I know what I want."

So he wasn't undecided about his food. Sorrell frowned at the scarcity of items on the menu, and she looked up as Theo ordered a diet cola.

"Same," she said.

"Ready to order?"

"Yes," Theo said. "I want the sirloin, medium-rare, please."

The waiter nodded and said, "The market price on that is sixty-seven dollars."

"Fine," Theo said, and they both looked at her.

Sixty-seven dollars for steak and mashed potatoes? Sorrell just blinked.

"She'll have the egg roll appetizers," Theo said. "As a meal, and she wants the beet and goat cheese salad. I'm guessing on the raspberry vinaigrette?" He raised his eyebrows, and Sorrell had the wherewithal to nod.

Theo nodded too, and so did the waiter, and with all that nodding going on, Sorrell finally found her voice.

"Where are you working now?" she asked, handing the waiter the menu so he could walk away.

"I'm not," he said. "I quit my job today. That's why I'm here."

"Oh." So many more questions began streaming

through her head, but Sorrell couldn't latch on to only one for long enough to speak it.

The waiter returned with their drinks, and Theo calmly unwrapped his straw. He wasn't offering up any other conversation handholds, and awkwardness raced through Sorrell.

"What are your plans?" she asked. Chestnut Springs was having a bachelor auction next week, and she needed more men. Maybe Theo…

Suddenly, the thought of anyone else going out with him revolted her.

"I have no plans," he said. "Right now. I'm going to plan a vacation when I go back to my room."

"I know Seth Johnson is looking for a couple of guys at Chestnut," she said. That would keep Theo close, and Sorrell began to wonder if they could simply go back to the way things used to be between them.

"I'll call him," Theo said, picking up his glass to take a drink.

"I miss you," she blurted out, her emotions surging. "I hate that I don't see you every day, and I hate that I lost my best friend."

Theo froze, his glass of cola halfway to his mouth. It seemed to take great effort for him to lift his eyes to meet hers, and Sorrell's hands shook as she reached for her own drink.

"Come back, Theo," she said. "Even if you can't come to Fox Hollow, come to Chestnut. You'll be close, and I'll ask you out a hundred times. Two hundred times—until you say yes."

She had no idea where the words had come from. Perhaps they had existed inside her all this time, and she simply hadn't realized it.

What was more true was probably that she'd simply been terrified to let them out of the box where she'd been storing them. Sorrell had spent a lot of time afraid of a lot of things.

She didn't want to do that anymore, especially with Theo.

"So if you come back," she said when he remained silent. "Would you go to dinner with me?"

He finally continued the trajectory of his glass and took a sip of his soda through the straw. "We're at dinner together right now."

"So you wouldn't go out with me again?"

"Depends."

"On what?"

"On how well this date goes," he said, stirring the straw around and making the ice cubes clink against the glass. "That's how dating works, Sorrell. If the first date goes well, you ask for a second one."

"Is this a first date then?"

He lifted one powerful shoulder in a shrug. "Up to you."

"No," she said. "I don't want things to be up to me." She made so many decisions at work as it was. She just wanted someone to tell her what to do with the rest of her life.

Seren had tried to tell Sorrell exactly what to do—*ask*

him. She could practically hear her sister's voice in her ears right then.

She had asked him.

He hadn't come right out and said yes. She suddenly knew how much courage it took to ask someone out, and how nerve-racking it was when they acted like they didn't want to go.

She'd not only acted like that, but she'd rejected him so many times.

"Did Sarena have her baby?" Theo asked, and Sorrell's whole soul lit up.

"Yes," she said. "She did."

"What did she name him?"

"West," she said. "He's so great, Theo." Sorrell didn't want to emit a wistful sigh, but it was very hard work to hold it back.

"I bet he is." Theo smiled then, and it was so devastatingly handsome that Sorrell let out a different kind of sigh. To get a grip on herself, she too reached for her straw and busied herself with her soda.

"Where did you go?" she asked.

"The Singer Ranch," he said, and the conversation picked up from there. Before she knew it, Sorrell and Theo had fallen right back into their old ways.

She could tease him, and he'd laugh. He could say something serious to her, and she'd watch him to make sure she knew how he felt about something.

She knew one thing—she really liked Theo, and she'd

been an absolute idiot by refusing him for so long that he wouldn't ask again.

Finally, he tossed some money on the table, and they slid out of the booth. It was likely way past Sorrell's bedtime, but she felt like she'd been hooked to an IV filled with energy drinks.

"I've been waiting for you to ask me out again," she said, linking her arm through his. "I was going to say yes." She looked up at him, but he didn't meet her eye. "You didn't ask again."

"A man can only hear no so many times," he murmured.

"I'm sorry," she said. "I was in a bad place for so long, and that put you in a bad place, and it just never lined up."

They went to the elevators to the left of the restaurant, and he put in his keycard to be able to call the car.

"Apology accepted," he said, but he did not offer her his arm again or take her hand in his. They got on the elevator together, and she pushed the nine while he pressed the twenty-seven.

"Wow," she said. "Staying on the top floor."

He gave her that smile again, and she wondered if he practiced it in the mirror at night. He had to, because it was so perfect. "Yes," he said. "I rented a suite, because I might be here a while."

Sorrell wanted to know why. She wanted to know how he could afford to stay in a hotel this nice for "a while."

She also did not want to get off on the ninth floor without knowing when she'd see him again, and he still had not accepted any of her invitations.

The elevator dinged on nine, and Sorrell looked at Theo. Theo gazed down at her.

Sorrell did the very first thing that came to her mind. She stepped into Theo's personal space, ran her fingers up the sides of his face, and drew him down to her level for a kiss.

"And you'll never guess who's here, Ma," he said, standing in front of the window on the twenty-seventh floor, his steaming coffee mug in one hand and his phone in the other.

"In Austin? Lord, I don't know anyone in Austin."

His mother hadn't left Georgia for a decade, that was true. In fact, she barely left the house. "Who?"

"Sorrell Adams," he said, lifting his mug to his lips. They were already curved, and Theo once again found his brain giving him a stern lecture. He could not allow himself to get swept up in the fantasy of him and Sorrell. She could change her mind on a dime—he'd seen her do it before.

"Sorrell—oh my," Ma said, and she started twittering the way she did when Theo brought up his love life.

"Calm down, Ma," he said, chuckling.

"You're going to give me a heart attack, boy," she said. "First, you quit your job. Then you go to Austin. And now we're back to Sorrell?"

"I never went away from Sorrell," Theo said.

"Yes, you did," Ma said. "You quit at that perfectly good ranch just to get away from her."

Theo sighed, because he couldn't really argue with her. Even she didn't know about his money, and Theo steered the conversation away from Sorrell and toward his mother's roof. "It's gonna rain soon," he said. "Did you get it fixed?"

"Yes, Willie and his son came and did it just a few days ago."

"Oh, Willie, huh?" Theo asked, smiling. He'd met the older gentleman who lived down the street from his mother.

The thought of her dating someone made Theo's heart expand a couple of sizes, as she'd really had a rough time in the companionship department. Her first husband had died very young in a car accident. She'd been left alone with two children.

She'd gotten remarried, but she couldn't have more children. She and Theo's father had adopted Theo when he was three years old. He couldn't remember life when he wasn't with Ma and Daddy, but Daddy had died when he was fourteen.

Then he'd met his biological father after the man had contacted Theo thirteen years ago. He'd known him for just over a year, and when Harvey Winters had passed away, Theo had inherited millions of dollars. Three hundred million dollars.

Theo had spent most of the last year of Harvey's life with him, learning about stocks and trading and investments. He'd done that for a solid year before he'd started working ranches, first in South Carolina, then Kentucky, and finally in Texas.

Time passed, and investments grew, and Theo had over a billion dollars in the bank now. He could picture Harvey's face, and he knew his father would be proud of him.

"I have to go, Ma," he said. "I love you."

"Love you too," she said. "Say hi to Sorrell for me."

"I sure will." Theo ended the call and watched out the window for a while longer. The park below the hotel wasn't filling quickly, as it was a weekday and people in Austin had jobs to get to.

Theo stepped off the elevator on the ninth floor at precisely eight o'clock. He turned left and went down the hall a few steps before Sorrell exited her room. Today, she wore a navy blue pencil skirt that accentuated her curves and made Theo's step less sure.

A white blouse paired well with the skirt, and Sorrell wore heels to complete the professional—yet still fantastically sexy—outfit.

"Morning, Sorrell," he said, feeling the need to sweep his cowboy hat off his head. He didn't, because he wasn't sure why he would. His fingers twitched as she gave him a quick smile and turned to tug on the door handle to make sure the door closed all the way.

When she could give him her full attention, she did, saying, "Good morning, Theo."

"You look amazing," he said, sliding his hands into his jeans pockets so he wouldn't wrap her in his arms. She looked like she might allow him to, though.

"Thank you," she said, her smile made of professionalism and kindness. "You look nice too."

"Nice?" The word came out of his mouth before he could censor himself. "I'll have to go shopping while you're in meetings today."

Sorrell laughed, her long hair falling over her shoulders and down her back as she tilted her head back. "Yeah? Why's that?"

"A man wants to look better than *nice*," he said, somewhat disgusted. "I get it. I only own jeans and these long-sleeved, plaid shirts."

Sorrell tiptoed her fingers up the front of his shirt, touching each button. "They're very cowboy."

"I can be more than a cowboy," he said, wondering where the words had come from. He'd never gone to college. He'd never wanted to be more than a cowboy. Ever. The man who'd raised him and who Theo knew as his father had owned a hardware store in a tiny town at the base of the Blue Ridge Mountains.

Theo had never wanted a life beyond those mountains, and he'd thought he'd simply inherit the store and live life in Smokey Ridge.

But God had called him in a different direction. He'd started working for a rancher in Georgia once he'd graduated high school, because his mother had had to sell the hardware store to make ends meet after Daddy died. From there, Theo had learned everything he could about horses, cattle, fixing fences, and following directions.

"I don't want you to be more than a cowboy," Sorrell said, stepping into him. Theo still didn't put his arms around her.

"I'll still find something like a polo," he said. "Maybe a leather jacket."

"Oh, wow," Sorrell said, giggling. She linked her arm through his and together, they went back toward the elevator. "So, did you get your trip planned?"

Theo's mind blanked for a moment, and then he remembered he'd told her he was planning a trip while they ate dinner last night. "No," he said. "It was late when I got back to my room, and I just went to bed."

"So you called your mother this morning, then." She didn't phrase it as a question, and Theo smiled at her.

"You know me too well." He reached up to push the button, happy to have her at his side. "My mom says hi, by the way."

Sorrell perked right up then, and Theo could see the compassion on her face. "That's so sweet," she said. "How is she?"

"She's good," he said.

"Since you don't have a job, are you going to go visit her for the holidays?"

"No," Theo said, the word almost a bark as it came out of his mouth. He stepped onto the elevator, Sorrell going with him.

"You never go home for Christmas."

"I don't like Christmas," he said.

"What?" She let her arm drop from his and turned toward him as the elevator doors closed. "Who doesn't like Christmas?" She gaped at him, and though she was still flawless with her makeup perfect, and those pretty pink lips, Theo looked away from her. "I've never heard you say that."

"Yeah, well, probably because it garners a reaction like the one you just had."

"Why don't you like Christmas?"

"It's complicated," Theo said, unwilling to explain right now. He wanted the next two hours to be more about catching up with each other than a deep, meaningful conversation that would leave him exhausted and wondering if Sorrell would believe him.

"You've always participated in our traditions at the ranch."

An idea began to bubble in his brain, but Theo needed more time to work through it. "Yeah, because...just because I don't like Christmas doesn't mean I want to be alone that day either."

Sorrell blinked at him, clearly surprised. "So you'll call Seth today about a job at Chestnut?"

Theo hadn't actually given that another thought, but she'd brought it up twice. It did seem like she wanted him near her.

"Theo?"

The elevator arrived in the lobby, and they couldn't stand there, facing each other. Theo managed to get off, and Sorrell slipped her fingers into his.

"I'll think about Chestnut," he said to her, though he couldn't promise how much brainpower he could give the ranch next door to the one where he'd worked for seven years. Because right now, his mind was brewing on an idea to skip Christmas completely, just as he'd hoped when he'd quit The Singer Ranch.

But he wasn't going to skip the holiday alone—if he could figure out how to ask Sorrell to run away with him, at least for a couple of weeks.

CHAPTER 4

Sorrell tucked her hands into her jacket pockets. Though Austin wasn't necessarily cold, it was the end of November, and that meant the temperatures weren't at a summer level. She hated the cold with everything inside her, and Austin seemed to have wind blowing constantly.

Her teeth chattered as they walked down the street, though the sun was well overhead. For some reason, she couldn't think of anything to ask Theo, and he had fallen quiet too. He often did, and Sorrell reminded herself that they'd spent plenty of time together where they weren't constantly chattering.

Some of her favorite moments with Theo happened in complete silence. When he stood next to her at the kitchen sink and helped her clean up. When he pulled the chair out at the dining room table for her. When he collapsed on the couch with a sigh and she sat next to him, the TV on in front of them. He'd fall asleep, and she would just listen to the soft sound of him inhaling, smile during the pause, and wish she could tell him how she felt as he exhaled.

She'd done that now, and Sorrell had never been prouder of herself. She'd been up forever last night, because she'd texted Serendipity, her younger sister, and told her everything that had happened.

After texting for fifteen minutes, Seren had obviously woken up, because she'd called. Sorrell had been up for another forty-five minutes while she lay in bed, trying to riddle through what to do next.

Seren had said, "You already kissed him Sorrell. There's nothing to do next."

But Sorrell knew that wasn't true. Seren had kissed her now-fiancé and then not known what to do. In fact, they'd broken up again after that.

Theo stepped in front of her and opened the door to Heavenly Hash, holding it for Sorrell to enter before him. She met his eye as she passed, and he kicked a smile at her that made her heart flop around a little harder.

He held up two fingers, and they followed a woman with her auburn hair in a high ponytail to a table in the middle of the crowded restaurant. Sorrell didn't like the crowds of people, and she was once again reminded of why she didn't live in the city. In fact, Chestnut Springs was starting to get too big for her, and she preferred to cook at home or order something out to the ranch over actually sitting down at a restaurant in town.

Sorrell relaxed as the heat in the restaurant started to

warm her, and as Theo opened his menu, he asked, "What are you looking forward to this Christmas, Sorrell?"

His question took her back for a moment, and she focused on shedding her jacket and picking up her menu too. "Mostly for it to be over, I guess," she said. "We're doing a bachelor auction at the community center next weekend, so I'll be working another seven days in a row. And then, as soon as that's over, we'll tear down our Thanksgiving display and put up the gingerbread house contest entries." She sighed just thinking about it. "I'll probably have to help with one or two of the two dozen trees we put around the center." She looked over the top of her menu and met Theo's gaze. "I hate the feel of those fake trees on my arms."

He gave her a small, kind smile. "I remember. Last year, I set up the tree while you directed me which boughs to bend up or down."

Sorrell's memory fired, and that was another tender moment between her and Theo. "Do you remember how red my arms were? I think I'm allergic to it."

"You'll have to wear long sleeves at work that day," he said, glancing back down at the menu.

"Or take my lunch," she said, only half kidding.

Theo chuckled, and Sorrell's eyes landed on the western hash. With the red peppers, onions, sausage, ham, and bacon, her taste buds started rejoicing. A waitress arrived, and they put in their orders. With the menus gone, Sorrell had nothing else to focus on.

Neither did Theo.

Something charged passed between them, and Sorrell

wasn't sure she liked it. She did, in that her attraction to Theo was just as strong as it had ever been. But she didn't, because things between them felt awkward now, as they often had after she'd rejected his dinner invitations in the past.

"What about you?" she asked. "I think we have a couple of hours to cover your complicated feelings about Christmas." She watched him, and Theo's eyebrows drew down slightly.

He shifted in his seat and cleared his throat, about as worked up as she'd ever seen him get.

"My dad died the day before Christmas," he said.

Something clicked in Sorrell's mind, and she cocked her head to the side, something not quite lining up. "Didn't you once do a video chat with your mom on the anniversary of your dad's death? That was in the summer..." She let her sentence hang there, sure she remembered that correctly. It had been summertime, because her father had died near summer months too, and it was something Theo had used to comfort her.

He cleared his throat again, and Sorrell had the distinct feeling he'd been lying to her all this time. Or was about to.

"That was my Daddy," he said. "He died the summer before my freshman year. My biological dad died the day before Christmas."

"Biological—" Sorrell cut off, her voice going mute as her brain took all of her energy to think.

"I was adopted when I was three," he said. "My biological father tracked me down in Kentucky when I was twenty-

Sorrell giggled, thinking that was at least better than being on the verge of tears all the time.

* * *

"You're late," Lance hissed a couple of hours later.

Sorrell slid into the seat beside him and whispered, "What did I miss?"

"Absolutely nothing," he said in a bored voice. He tilted his notebook toward her. "Well, I did manage to do a little shading."

Sorrell looked at the doodles on his notebook, where he'd drawn a grid with dozens of smaller squares inside. He'd shaded in every other one. "That's what you've done in the last twenty minutes?"

"Someone had to get here early to get these amazing seats," he whispered back. "There are people standing in the back, Sorrell."

She twisted and looked over her shoulder. She felt like since Theo had come back into her life, she didn't notice much of anything—except him. He dominated everything, and knowing he was here in the hotel made focusing on the new password reset for guests downright yawn-worthy.

"Thank you, Lance."

"So...out with your boyfriend?"

Sorrell simply shook her head, though she made no effort to conceal her smile.

"Oh, that grin says yes," Lance said. "I'll have you know I was out quite late too." He hit the T's on the last few words pretty hard. "That hostess knew a great late-night place to get cupcakes."

"Sure," Sorrell said, rolling her eyes. "Cupcakes, Lance? Really?"

"Honest," he said. "It was a food truck on Sixth."

"I can't believe you went to Sixth," Sorrell hissed. "It's crazy-town down there at night." She'd specifically been told —by Lance himself—not to go anywhere in Austin alone after dark. It wasn't a particularly violent city, but it was the City of Weird—and for good reason.

"I would never let you go," he said. "Without me, at least. I could take you tonight?" He lifted his eyebrows, but Sorrell shook her head.

"Another date with Mister Tall, Dark, and Broody?" Lance chuckled, and the woman sitting in front of them turned around.

Embarrassment filled Sorrell, and she ducked her head. How that other woman could concentrate on the boring presentation on the screen up front, Sorrell didn't know.

Yes, she had another date with Theo that night. She'd asked him again—suggested dinner, really. She'd suggested they get together after her conference. He'd said yes. He'd find a great restaurant, and he'd meet her in the lobby at seven.

Sorrell wasn't entirely sure what would happen in a couple of days when her conference ended. It was only an hour's drive back to Chestnut Springs, but that felt like another planet entirely right now.

Theo had not said a word about Chestnut Ranch or

calling Seth. She hadn't asked how he could stay in this hotel, jobless, and afford it.

As she suffered through the meeting, she had the very real feeling that in two days' time, she'd be driving back to the ranch while Theo went back to the twenty-seventh floor. They'd be apart again, and Sorrell's heart twitched in her chest.

Emotion surged in the back of her throat, and she tried desperately to swallow it back.

She wanted Theo back in her life for good. She didn't want to drive away from him, wondering when she'd see him again.

Two days, she thought. She had two days to figure out a way to get him to come back to Chestnut Springs with her— hopefully to stay.

Her pulse quivered in her neck, because she knew she would not survive another separation from Theo Lange. *Please, please*, she prayed as the presenter droned on and on about the new secure features of the software the community center would be implementing in the new year. *Please bless me to be able to say the right thing to Theo so we can be together after this weekend.*

CHAPTER 5

Theo picked up the printouts from the color printer in the executive business lounge on the twenty-seventh floor and looked at them.

A smile worked its way through his whole soul. Yes, the mountains were what he needed. And not just hills, like what he lived in and grown up in around Texas or Georgia.

Real mountains.

The Rocky Mountains.

Snow, and a cabin tucked in the woods. With a burning fire, and hot chocolate and coffee, and popcorn. Fuzzy socks and icicles, and the rest of the world on the outside.

Beaver Creek, Colorado would give him all of those things. He'd found a cabin he could rent for the next six weeks, and he'd already called to book it. The three-bedroom house was made of logs and had a furnace as well as a wood-burning stove.

The roads were plowed in the winter, and he could easily

get there in a two-day drive, unpack his stuff and skip the whole month of December. Part of January too.

He looked up from the papers depicting the cabin, which was a short twenty-five-minute drive from a village that had everything he'd need. Small grocery store, post office, even a row of restaurants. He could buy firewood there, rent snowmobiles or snowshoes, and even get a post office box if he wanted.

Theo just needed Sorrell to go with him. He couldn't stand the thought of leaving the hotel and simply driving back to Chestnut Springs. He could call Seth, sure. He could get a job at the ranch. And eventually, he'd probably do both of those things.

But right now, Theo just needed an escape.

The only thing he didn't want to leave behind right now was Sorrell Adams.

He drew in a long breath and held it, a tactic he used to force his thoughts to slow down. He'd been jumping back and forth from one side of the fence to the other all day.

Ask her.

Don't ask her.

Text her right now.

Don't bring it up at all.

His doubts could really grow teeth sometimes, and Theo had been unhooking them all day. His phone chimed, and he pulled it out of his pocket to check it.

In the lobby, Sorrell had texted, and Theo hurried out of the executive lounge. As he strode down the hallway, he tucked the papers under one arm so he could use both hands to send her a response.

On my way. Be down as fast as the elevator moves.

Thirty seconds later, he emerged into the lobby of the hotel, and much to his disgust, a man sat at the grand piano playing Christmas songs.

He glared at the guy, though he was just doing his job, and swept the area for Sorrell. He found her standing several paces away, her back to him, wearing a stunning pencil skirt that accentuated all of her curves. She'd tucked a pale pink blouse into the skirt, and her dark hair fell down her back.

His heart boomed a couple of times, because he was—and always had been—attracted to her physically. Even when he wanted to stay away because she hurt his feelings, he couldn't. She turned and looked over her shoulder, and Theo got his legs moving again.

She caught sight of him, instant recognition lighting those gorgeous eyes and causing a smile to lift the corners of her mouth.

"Hey," he said, tucking his phone away as he arrived. He folded the papers into fourths and tucked them in his back pocket too.

"What's that?" she asked.

"Something for later." With his hands free, he took one of hers in his and stepped even closer to her. He wasn't sure exactly what he was doing, but his other hand came up and pressed on her back, bringing her right against him. He took a deep breath of her, the scent of roses and perfume and dryer sheets entering his nose.

He exhaled, and all of the doubts he'd been battling that day quieted. His pulse calmed. He stepped back and smiled at her. "It's so good to see you."

She ducked her head too, her smile only increasing. "What have you done today?"

"Oh, I went to the park," he said casually, turning to lead her toward the exit. "What are you feeling like for dinner?"

"Anything," she said. "You said you had a place picked out."

"Did I?"

She giggled, and Theo liked the thread of desire that pulled through him with the sound. "Yes, you did. This afternoon. In a text. I can show you if you want."

"I got it," he said, stepping through the automatic doors. He liked that he and Sorrell weren't dating in Chestnut Springs. They'd needed a fresh start, and perhaps this could be it. Outside, he drew in another long breath. "It's a great place that serves upscale diner food."

"Sounds great," she said. "I could use a hearty plate of buttermilk pancakes after the meetings I've had today."

"You had time to go upstairs and change," he said. "That bad?"

"Just boring," she said. "It's a new software system. It's not hard to figure out which buttons to click to get a new user in."

"I can't imagine," he said.

"We're one of the first implementing it," she said. "So they'll be improving their training from our feedback."

"Mm." He handed his ticket to the valet and looked at

her. She seemed happy, though Sorrell always had a generally positive air about her. Her emotions swam right near the surface, and they always had. Theo had seen her cry countless times, and she wasn't always super sad when she did. When Sorrell needed to release something, that energy came out in the form of tears.

"Looks like you went shopping today too," she said, running her free hand up the sleeve of his leather jacket. "It's...nice."

"Ho, hokay," he said with a chuckle. "I see how this is going to be."

She grinned at him and leaned right into him. Theo held his ground, because while he'd seen the spark of attraction in Sorrell's gaze before, it had never been quite this vibrant. "It's going to be fun," she said. "Diner food with a hot cowboy."

"I suppose that's better than *nice*," he said, though he was too old to be called hot. He reached up and ran his hand down both sides of his beard. "You never said if you liked the beard."

"It's different," she said. "A good kind of different."

"Needed a change," he said, already stepping onto dangerous ground and they hadn't even left the hotel yet.

Sorrell shuttered something behind the mask that slid onto her face, and she looked away. "Everyone needs a change from time to time."

His truck pulled up before he could answer, and Theo's chest squeezed as he held the door for Sorrell as she climbed into the truck in that skinny skirt. He felt like a giant had pinned him to the ground and was gradually putting a bit more weight on his lungs with every passing moment.

He wasn't even sure why.

He got behind the wheel and he kept the conversation light on the way to the diner. Stuff about the ranch, and Sarena, and her cat. Stuff they could chitchat about forever. Stuff that didn't really matter.

Once they had a table in the long train car that was the diner, and Sorrell had stopped exclaiming about how "vintage" and "adorable" the place was, Theo took a moment to look at the menu.

"Not Your Momma's Tuna Casserole," he read. "Reimagined Salisbury Steak. Two-Thousand-And-Patty-Melt." He looked up at Sorrell, a measure of delight moving through him. "I think this all sounds amazing."

"Is this going to be one of those times where you order more than one thing?" She grinned at him, clearly flirting with him.

"I mean, maybe," he said, looking down again. "Did you see they have spaghetti and meatballs?"

"No," she said. "They have Unretro Meatballs and Spaghetti."

Theo chuckled, because yeah, that's what it was called. New Age Meatloaf and Mash sounded good to him, as did the Joke's On You Chicken Pot Pie. Surrounding that part of the menu were a ton of *Why did the chicken cross the road?* jokes.

Theo was so glad the concierge had suggested this place. He had spent the morning in the park and at the mall. Then he'd stopped by the concierge desk, showered, and started searching for his holiday getaway.

A waitress arrived wearing a pink and white dress, and they put in their soda and food orders.

"I can't believe you got the Next Level Onion Rings," Sorrell said as the woman walked away with their menus. "And the New Age Meatloaf and Mash, *and* the Two-Thousand-and-Patty-Melt."

"I'm hungry," he said, leaning back in the booth.

She laughed and shook her head.

"You'll eat a ton of the onion rings anyway, sugar," he said. "I know what you like." Their eyes met, and Theo darn near got electrocuted by the energy snapping between them. He cleared his throat and sat up straight. "If I show you something, will you promise to listen all the way to the end?"

Sorrell straightened her shoulders too, as if she were preparing to get in a boxing ring and fight for her life. She sobered, but none of the electricity flowing around them lessened. "I can commit to that."

Slowly, Theo reached into his back pocket and took out the papers. He unfolded them, his head down, the brim of his cowboy hat between him and Sorrell. "Remember I said I didn't like Christmas?"

"Yes."

"And that I just wanted to skip the whole thing this year?" He looked up, and Sorrell's eyes were glued to the papers still facing him. He turned them around. "I wasn't kidding about that. I need a break. I don't want to think about the holidays this year." He pushed the papers toward her. "I want to go here."

She glanced up at him quickly—long enough for him to see the questions in her eyes. She reached for the papers and pulled them right in front of her. "Beaver Creek," she murmured as she read the paper. A few seconds later, she turned the top page over, and the pictures of the cabin, the pine trees, and the snow filled the next couple of pages.

"This place is really nice, Theo," she said, passing the papers back to him.

He didn't touch them or look at them, but maintained eye contact with her. "Remember how I said I didn't like being alone on Christmas either?"

The waitress arrived with their drinks, and Sorrell practically dove for her lime Rickey. Maybe that was the answer to his implied question. A pinch tugged in Theo's chest, and his throat stuck together it was so dry. He'd ordered a diet cola, and he flashed a smile at the waitress as she dropped straws on the table and said, "Food's almost up."

How that could be possible, Theo wasn't sure. They'd ordered maybe five minutes ago.

He took a long drag of his soda and swallowed, letting the carbonation burn the whole way into his stomach.

"I want you to come with me," he said. "The cabin's plenty big enough. The bedrooms are all on a different floor. My truck will easily navigate those roads." He stopped, because she'd already started shaking her head no.

"I can't just come with you, Theo," she said, glancing

around as if her mother would be there to tell her how inappropriate such a trip would be.

"Why not?" he asked. "I'll be a perfect gentleman. Have I ever not been a perfect gentleman with you?"

"It's not that," she said, her eyes round. "I have a job. I can't just leave it. And I cook Christmas dinner. And Christmas Eve dinner. I can't just leave my sisters."

Theo waited a moment to see what else she'd say. When she remained quiet, he said. "Sure you can. You can leave all of that. Your sisters won't die if you don't make a ham."

"They might," she said, her fingers worrying against the straw wrapper. "I can't just quit my job." She peered at him, her eyes narrowing a little. "How can you? How can you afford this hotel? How can you take the next six weeks off?"

So she'd seen the dates on the paper. Theo would've actually been disappointed if she hadn't. If she'd seen those, she'd surely have seen he'd already booked it and paid for it. And that he'd be checking in on Tuesday.

"No job to come back to," she continued. "I know you didn't call Seth today. That jacket probably cost a few hundred dollars." She pulled in a breath, which got her to stop talking.

Theo gazed at her calmly, because he'd been keeping this secret from her for far too long as it was.

"I don't need to work," he said, his voice almost a monotone. "I have plenty of money."

"Is that so?" Sorrell settled back into the booth and folded her arms. "I might need you to define what 'plenty' means to you."

Theo took another drink of his soda. "Enough that I could buy the whole town of Beaver Creek," he said. "With cash." Now that he'd practically told her of his independent wealth, a whole bunch of words crowded in his throat to get out.

He held them back though, because while he knew Sorrell could burst into tears at any moment, he also knew she needed a few seconds to process things. So he'd wait and see what she said next—at least as long as he could.

CHAPTER 6

Sorrell's brain couldn't grab onto one thought or question and vocalize it. She blinked at Theo, trying to figure out what to say.

"So much that you'd never have to work again if you didn't want to," he said. "So much that I could buy a ranch twenty times bigger than The Singer Ranch, staff it, and never have to sell a single cow—and still have money."

"So you're rich like Darren."

"Yes," he said simply.

"Why have you been working at Fox Hollow for seven years then?" Why would someone do that? Ranching wasn't easy work, she knew that. She'd hated it with every fiber of her being, but she'd helped her parents around the farm plenty of times growing up. More than she ever liked.

Theo just shrugged, and Sorrell tried to imagine what life would be like if she didn't have to work. She'd tend to the gardens surrounding the farmhouse, and read in the middle of the day, and have copious amounts of time to try new recipes.

She could throw a dinner party every weekend, and get her hair done without being in a rush. So many things came to mind—and not one of them was finding a job so she had to fit life in around work.

"I don't even know what to say," she said.

"I said I'd think about Chestnut," he said. "Say you'll think about Beaver Creek." He picked up the papers, refolded them, and put them back in his pocket.

"You're going Tuesday."

"Monday, actually," he said. "It's a two-day drive up there. I'll get a hotel somewhere on the way."

"Oh, of course." She looked away, unsure about why her emotions were quivering so close to crying. The tears were there though, right behind her eyes, already desperate to come out.

"Sorrell, does it upset you that I'm rich?"

She couldn't look at him, and she wasn't even sure why. Thankfully, their food arrived, and wow, there was so much of it. The menu hadn't been lying when it said the portions were from a momma's kitchen trying to fatten up her kids, because her Caesar salad was piled high on a plate easily as big as a hubcap, and the Unretro Meatballs and Spaghetti came in a bowl that Sorrell would more correctly label a trough.

"Holy cow," Theo said with a laugh. The tension at their

table broke, but that only made Sorrell want to cry too. She swiped at her eyes while Theo picked up a giant-sized napkin and laid it on his lap.

She would not ruin her makeup over this. She wasn't even sure why she was emotional at all. If there was anything she should be feeling, it should be elation. The man she liked was rich. Really rich, by the sound of it. Why should that upset her?

She picked up her fork and managed to toss a smile at Theo before digging into her salad. The parmesan cheese had been shaved in wonderfully thick slices, and she put one with a tiny bit of lettuce in her mouth. The salty flavor made everything inside her sigh with happiness, and when she looked at Theo again, her emotions were finally in check.

He paused when their eyes met, his question still hanging in the air between them.

"A little," she said.

"Why?" He nudged the tower—a literal *tower*—of onion rings toward her. She reached for one, because she did enjoy an onion ring dipped in barbecue sauce about as much as she liked candy. Maybe more.

"I don't know," she admitted. "Maybe because you're already so perfect, and to find out you're rich too is a little overwhelming."

Theo burst out laughing, but Sorrell hadn't been trying to be funny. She dipped her onion ring while his laughter filled the diner, and crunched her way through a bite or two until he sobered.

"I am not perfect," he said.

"Good," she said. "Because neither am I, and it's...maybe I just feel a little inferior to you." She hadn't even realized she felt that way until she vocalized the words.

"That can't be true," he said, his expression revealing how surprised he was. His eyebrows were up and everything. "Have you eaten what you've cooked? You work an insane schedule, and still come home and cook, take care of your sisters, and always have time to talk to anyone. I don't know how you do it."

"That's just because you don't like talking to people."

"No," he said. "I don't. Except for you. I like talking to you."

Sorrell ducked her head and finished her onion ring. The man gave great compliments, whether he knew it or not.

"So you'll think about it?"

"I'll think about it," she said. "You need an answer by Sunday?"

"Yeah," he said. "Because if you're not going to come, I can head north from here. If you are, I have to follow you back to Chestnut Springs and wait for you to pack."

"Even if I come, you'd have to do that," she said, alarms ringing inside her again. She'd seen those dates. January twelfth. She couldn't even imagine what she'd do in a cabin from December first to January twelfth.

She couldn't believe she was even considering going with him. She'd have to make so many explanations. To her sisters. Her boss. Everyone. The town had paid for her to come to this conference, and she was one of four directors at the community center. She was in charge of a big bachelor auction in just one week.

She couldn't just up and leave the state on Monday morning with Theo.

She couldn't.

That wasn't what adults did.

She put a smile on her face, though, because she didn't want to spend the time she had with Theo worried and obsessing. If he'd be driving north on Monday while she drove south, she wanted to enjoy every minute she had with him until then.

* * *

"What did you tell him?" Serendipity asked later that night.

"I said I'd think about it."

"Are you thinking about it?" Sarena asked.

Sorrell gazed out her window, wondering what the view was like from twenty more floors up. Probably amazing. Spectacular. The entire downtown skyline of Austin.

"How can I *not* think about it?" Sorrell asked. "I could take my own car. Then I can leave when I want to. I could come back for Christmas with you guys. I don't need to go with him. Be trapped up there..." She trailed off, because while part of her did feel trapped, another part of her thought that sounded romantic.

Snowed in with Theo.

She shivered, though she'd turned her heat up the moment she'd returned from dinner.

"You should absolutely take your own car," Seren said.

"Seren," Sarena admonished. Her baby fussed in the background, and Sorrell's heart squeezed. She didn't want to miss West's first Christmas.

He's not your baby, she told herself. Sarena and Darren would be making their own memories this holiday. Brian and Serendipity would too. Maybe Sorrell should as well...

"She's really got to think about this," Sarena said as if Sorrell weren't on the call anymore. "She's worked at the community center for over a decade. That's retirement, Sorrell. How can you quit?"

"Maybe they'll give me a personal leave," she said.

"Do they do that?" Serendipity asked.

"I've seen them do it," Sorrell said, though the leaves she knew about were because women had babies, or people left to go tend to their ill parents. Nine times out of ten, the person who'd taken a leave didn't return to the center.

If Theo was as rich as he said he was, Sorrell wouldn't need to return either.

Her stomach cramped and she sank onto the bed. "Only if you fall in love with him," she said.

"What?" Serendipity asked.

"Did you say you were in love with him?" Sarena asked.

"No," Sorrell said. "He said he's rich like Dareen, Sarena."

Silence came through the line, and that only spurred Sorrell's thoughts to come out of her mouth faster. "So I said, if I fall in love with him, I don't need a retirement. I don't need the job at the community center."

More silence, and Sorrell needed it to think. "I have to go," she said.

"No," Serendipity said. "Don't go. Keep talking."

"I need to think."

"Sorrell," Sarena said, but another long pause came through the line. Her oldest sister finally said, "Don't get too deep inside that brain of yours, okay? Make the column-chart if you need to. Whatever. Send me a picture, because West is super fussy right now, and I'm going to be up all night long." Another wail came through the line, nearly splitting Sorrell's eardrum.

"But stop at five things in each column," she said.

"Five?" Sorrell said. "That's impossible." She stepped over to the desk to find a notepad. Hotels always had them.

"Five," Sarena and Serendipity said together. "Other-wise," Seren continued. "You get freaked out, and you'll start crying."

"I'm not going to cry over this," Sorrell said. She'd made that promise to herself at dinner.

"Five things," Sarena said. "Promise me."

"Fine," Sorrell said, only to get her sisters off the call. Her skin itched. She needed to make her pros and cons chart right now. "I won't put more than five things in each column."

"Great," Sarena said. "Love you, Sorrell. Seren, sorry, can you? I have to feed him."

Scuffling and crying came through the line, and then

Serendipity said, "Personally, Sorrell, I think you should just go. Don't make the chart. Throw caution out the window and go with him."

Sorrell's throat closed, and she couldn't even respond. She wasn't the type of person who threw anything anywhere, unless it was a healthy pinch of salt into the caramel she was making to go over freshly popped popcorn.

"Just think about this for one second," Serendipity said, her voice low as if she was trying to keep Sarena from over-hearing. "You haven't seen him or spoken to him in weeks. You've been a wreck around the farmhouse, thinking you'd never see him again. And you run into him in Austin, of all places? While you're at a work conference?"

Sorrell could just imagine Serendipity shaking her head. "That's not coincidence, Sorrell. That's fate."

"It's not fate," Sorrell said, though she did love the romanticized idea of fate. Of some unknown force bringing her and Theo together, because they simply *belonged* together.

"Divine intervention, then," Serendipity said. "It's something, Sorrell. Even you can admit that."

"All right," Sorrell said. "I'll call you tomorrow."

"Love you."

"Love you too." Sorrell ended the call and looked at the long, tall pad of paper she'd found. Her mind moved quickly and seemed to stall all at the same time.

Instead of searching for a pen, she pulled open her laptop, sat down at the desk, and gave the machine a moment to connect to the Internet.

Then she searched for Beaver Creek cabins. Perhaps if she was armed with more knowledge about this place she'd be going, she could make a more informed decision as to whether she should say yes and skip Christmas with Theo...or not.

CHAPTER 7

'm in.

Theo stared at the text, sure he'd misinterpreted the four letters somehow. Maybe his mother had sent them.

Sorrell's name sat above the words. She'd sent the text. She hadn't specified what she was "in" on, but Theo knew.

He smiled as he held his phone above his face, as he hadn't gotten out of bed yet. She'd sent the text at nearly two o'clock in the morning, and a blip of guilt went out with every racing heartbeat that he'd kept her awake so long.

I want to take my own car, she'd said next. *And I can't come until after the bachelor auction. Sorry, but I just can't. It's in a week, and I'm in charge, and while I want to be spontaneous and fun, I also have to be a real adult.*

"Of course," he murmured to himself.

So I'll call my boss today, and I'm hoping to be in Beaver Creek on December 7.

Theo's heart thrashed in his chest, and he sat up to try to relieve some of the pressure. "I can't believe this." He just kept staring at the texts. Had someone stolen her phone? Maybe the soft, sensible Sorrell he knew had been replaced by her more adventurous sister, Serendipity.

Are you sure? He typed out the words and considered sending them. In the end, he deleted them off the message and wrote *Thank you, Sorrell.*

That sounded stupid too, and Theo stood and paced over to the window, his mind racing. He wanted Sorrell to come. He did. He'd wanted Sorrell for as long as he could remember. Why then, was his heartbeat pouncing and spitting in his chest?

He tapped to make a call, hoping it wasn't too early for his mother.

"Teddy," she said, one of the only people left in the world who called him that. She also sometimes said Theodore, which was his full legal name.

"Ma," he said, relief chasing away the doubt in his soul. "I have to run something by you."

"Go ahead, sugar," she said.

He pictured her on the big back deck he'd built for her five years ago when he'd gone to visit, a cup of tea beside her on the little round table she'd picked out at the hardware store. It was a peaceful scene, with a brilliant blue sky overhead.

"It's about Sorrell," he said. "I asked her to skip Christmas with me."

"Teddy," she said again, the tone completely different

"Still fine. You tell me when you can start, and I'll keep my temps on until then."

His stay at the cabin lasted until January twelfth. With driving time back... "January fifteenth," Theo said. "I'll be back in Texas by the fifteenth."

"Sounds great," Seth said. "I'm assuming you need lodging?"

"Yes, sir."

"You do not need to call me sir," Seth said with a laugh. "And are you wanting to work the ranch or work with the dogs?"

"Whatever you need," Theo said. "I like dogs just fine."

"Brian's moved over to dogs exclusively," he said. "His cabin is small, but we've put two people in there before. I keep telling Travis we need more cowboy cabins. We have so many more men with us now."

"I can get a place in town too," Theo said. "It just makes the wage higher."

"Let me talk to Trav," Seth said. "It's not for several weeks. I can let you know about that?"

"Sure," Theo said. If he needed time to find somewhere to live, he might not be able to start at Chestnut Ranch right on the fifteenth. He told himself to cross the bridge when he came to it, and the call with Seth ended amidst a flurry of barking and growling.

Suddenly, Theo wasn't so keen to work in the rescue dog operation. He should probably ask Brian about it. Pros and cons and all of that. Theo understood cattle. He knew how to check soil pH and deal with moody bulls. He'd done crop rotation and fence fixing and the dozens of other tasks it took to keep a ranch operational and functional.

He quickly thumbed a text to Seth. *You know what? I'd prefer to work on the ranch side.*

He might as well say what he really wanted. He'd learned that from Harvey in the short time they'd spent together. He stayed on the bench, basking in the weak winter sunlight, for just a few more minutes, thinking of the eleven months he'd spent with his biological father.

They'd been good months. Hard at times. He'd learned a lot about himself, that was for sure. Some things he'd wondered about—his almost clinical nature toward solving problems, for one—had become crystal clear when he'd seen someone else perceive and act the same way. Other things—his concern and care for others—had become even more baffling to him.

Harvey hadn't seemed to care about anyone but himself.

"That was why he was alone," Theo said to himself as he stood up. "Why none of his other children wanted to be around him. Why he tracked you down, and you spent his last days with him."

Theo hadn't figured that out until after Harvey's death, when he'd met the man's other four children at the funeral. His eldest daughter was two years older than Theo, and Virginia had taken control of everything once Harvey had taken his last breath.

Theo had called her, because Harvey had instructed him to. From there, Theo grieved on his own, in a unique way, for a man he'd barely known.

didn't feel like crying at the thought of Serendipity moving out of the farmhouse to live with Brian in the cabin they'd spent the last two months repairing and renovating.

She wasn't jealous of Sarena's life, with the husband and the baby and the brand-new house down the lane.

Happiness filtered through her, and she put a genuine smile on her face. "I love you guys," she whispered. "You too, baby West." She bent down and pressed her lips to the sleeping infant's forehead before looking at Sarena and Serendipity again.

"I can't believe you said yes," Sarena said with a smile. "I'm so glad you did, but you have to admit, it's a little shocking."

"I can admit that," Sorrell said, her familiar doubts making a reappearance. "Do you think it's a mistake?"

"Absolutely not," Serendipity said. "It's exactly what you and Theo need."

"He doesn't like Christmas," she said, her mind moving down that road again. "I think I'll miss it. Will you guys text me pictures of your stockings and trees and presents and all of that?"

"Sure," Sarena said. "You can still call us on Christmas too."

"Yeah," Serendipity said, grinning. "Just do it from your private level in that posh cabin." She nudged Sorrell with her shoulder, and all three of them laughed together.

Sorrell took a great big breath, her mind going in a lot of directions now. "I can't believe I'm doing this."

"It's going to be amazing," Sarena said. "I can't imagine

Theo's feelings for you have changed, and we all know he's been in love with you for years."

Sorrell pressed her lips together as she nodded. That was what Sarena had been telling her, at least. Even Serendipity had said she could see the way Theo looked at Sorrell. He had asked her out a whole lot. He even kissed her like he was utterly enamored with her.

Not that Sorrell would truly know, as she hadn't been out with a man she'd kissed in over a decade.

She'd held the belief that all cowboys had trouble running in their veins since her disastrous relationship with the man that had closed her heart off to the possibility of ever falling in love again.

Sorrell knew she needed to open the box inside her soul where she'd stored everything that had happened with Cameron Carlisle.

The cowboy had shown her exactly how many pieces a heart could break into, and precisely how long it took to put back together. She knew some of those pieces weren't back in their proper places, and they wouldn't be until she told Theo why she'd told him no so many times.

Good news, she told herself as Serendipity got up with the declaration that they needed ice cream. *You'll have five weeks alone with Theo to tell him everything.*

She wasn't sure if the rumble moving through her muscles was borne of excitement or terror, but it was there nonetheless.

CHAPTER 9

Theo checked the temperature on his dashboard as he made the turn as prompted by his navigation system. "Holy cow," he said under his breath. He was surprised he couldn't see that breath, because it was only eighteen degrees outside.

Eighteen.

Theo didn't even know what that felt like. Everything looked like a winter wonderland. Like the movies he'd watched as a kid, with blue icicles hanging from every eave, and couples bundled up as they ice skated to romantic music.

His system told him to turn left in one thousand feet, and when he did, the next thing he was told was, "Your destination is on the right."

He eased to a stop and peered to the right, out the passenger-side window. The three-story cabin stood there, the huge windows on the front of it reflecting back the sunlight bearing down on Beaver Creek that afternoon.

A sense of happiness filled Theo. He'd made it. Not only that, but he felt like he was finally exactly where he was supposed to be.

That made no sense, but he swung his truck into the gravel driveway of the cabin, which someone had recently pushed the snow out of. Before killing the engine and getting out, he checked his email.

Thankfully, he got a signal up here, and he was able to get to the email with the entrance instructions.

"They'll have the heater on for me..." He scanned for the code. "Okay, four, four, six, nine." He looked up at the house, thinking he better make a run for it so he didn't freeze to death.

He currently had everything he owned with him, but it didn't need to be brought in all at once. He grabbed the bag he'd used at the hotel as he got out of the truck, and nothing froze as he went up the steps to the main level entrance, where the lockbox was located.

With the code in, the box revealed the key, and Theo entered to a warm, cozy cabin. Additional joy filled him, and he couldn't help smiling as he explored the place. On a Tuesday afternoon, he wondered if Sorrell could take a video call, and he texted her to ask.

While he waited for her to answer, he went out to the truck and brought in the new towels he'd bought. The bedding. The groceries he'd picked up in a town at the base of the canyon. With everything else loaded into the house, he just needed to know where to put it all.

His phone rang, and he swiped on a call from Sorrell. "You made it to the cabin, I'm assuming," she said.

"I did," he said. "Wondering if you wanted a virtual tour so you could pick your bedroom."

"You sound happy," she said. "Must be a nice place."

"It is," he said.

"You pick for me," she said.

"I think you'll want the third floor," he said. "I've already been through the house. It has a loft, with all the light coming in from the windows. And it's the only bedroom with an attached bathroom. I can take the basement." She'd probably freeze to death down there anyway. It had been noticeably cooler than the main level and the third floor, and even Theo would need a space heater if the furnace couldn't keep the basement warm.

"Okay," she said. "Whatever you're comfortable with."

"I think that's the best way to go," he said, looking at the bedroom down the hall from the kitchen. The bathroom sat right across from the pantry, and he wondered if he could just take the bed and bath on this level.

No, they'd agreed to each have a level and then share the main.

"I'm sorry, Theo," she said in a hushed voice. "I have to go. I'll call you tonight, okay?"

"Okay," he said, and she was gone in the next moment.

Theo drew in a deep breath and held it. He wasn't going to be angry she was being responsible and finishing up a huge event at the community center. "She'll be here in a week," he told himself. "Less than that. Six days."

He needed to learn the lay of the land by then. Visit the shops and stores down in Beaver Creek. He could time how long it took to get to the movie theater. He wanted to check out the stores down in the town at the base of the canyon and learn the best snowshoe trails.

That way, when Sorrell arrived, he'd be ready to show her around.

He set about unpacking the food he'd bought. Then he stripped the beds and took everything down to the laundry room in the basement. He remade the beds with the new sheets and quilts and returned to the kitchen to read through the binder of information on the counter.

He learned how to adjust the temperature in the cabin, and how to start the wood-burning stove. He looked through the closets and pantry and found movies, games, and a few staples.

Yes, he could have an amazing time here—even if he was alone.

But he didn't have to be alone, and Theo took a second and closed his eyes. "Thank you, Lord. For Sorrell."

His simple prayer of gratitude buoyed his spirits, and he whistled to himself as he went around the house and removed the little knickknacks that looked like anything remotely holiday-related.

Pine trees could be Christmas trees, and Theo didn't need to think of that every time he looked at the mantle. The little trees there were really candles, and he wouldn't be using them anyway.

Once the whole cabin was completely Christmas-free, Theo stood in the main room and looked around. "This is going to be the best vacation ever," he promised himself. A smile filled his soul, and Theo went downstairs to test out the water pressure in the shower in the basement bathroom.

The following morning, Theo scrambled eggs for himself, thinking of where he'd been only a few days ago. Crammed in a cowboy cabin with people he barely knew. He much preferred this, and he hadn't even realized how stifled he'd been at The Singer Ranch.

Satisfied with everything at the cabin, Theo got behind the wheel of his truck again, thinking everything in his life would be better if he had a dog he could spend time with.

He let himself mull over the idea as he made the drive, and he marveled at the beauty of ice and snow, and how the pavement shone like black gold in the sunlight.

He'd seen the roads in Georgia like this growing up too, and the sight caused a smile to fill him. Again.

He couldn't believe how much happier he was here than he'd been only a few days ago on The Singer Ranch. Why it had taken him so long to act, he didn't know.

"Probably because you didn't know where you're supposed to be." He still didn't know.

He wasn't a particularly religious man, but as he rolled

into the quaint mountain town, his thoughts turned more inward to his soul. He wasn't quite sure how to talk to God, but he simply said, "Thank you for bringing me here."

He navigated to the movie theater and found several cars in the lot. It looked like a newer building, with an attached bowling alley and indoor laser tag. That all sounded fun, and if he and Sorrell needed to get out of the cabin, there was something to do nearby.

His heart beat irregularly for a moment, and Theo still couldn't believe Sorrell was going to come. He hated that she had to make the drive herself, but then he reminded himself that she was a capable woman.

She didn't think herself strong, but Theo knew she was. She dealt with difficult personalities at work. She had a strong bond with her sisters, and she'd had to figure out her own place among them once they started finding significant others. That had been hard for her, and Theo had been by her side every step of the way.

Almost, he thought. *Until you left the ranch.*

A slip of regret moved through him, but he capped it. He'd had to act in his own best interest, and he didn't need to apologize for it. Just like skipping Christmas. He didn't have to justify what he was doing. He needed to do it, and that had to be good enough.

He drove toward the grocery store again, because it sat at the end of Main Street, which he'd wanted to drive down. The cabin had mentioned it as one of the oldest in Colorado and worth a visit.

CHAPTER 10

Sorrell's soul lit up when her phone showed Theo's name on the screen. She'd just lived through the longest week of her life, and not only because she'd slept less than she had in years.

"Hey," she said, hearing faint yipping in the background. He'd adopted three puppies last week, and a morning hadn't passed since where she didn't wake up to a dozen pictures of them. They made her smile, because they made Theo so happy.

"Where are you?" he asked.

"I just got to Beaver Creek. I'm getting gas and some groceries, and I'll be there." Excitement tripped through her, just as it had been for the past two days as she'd driven farther north than she'd ever gone. "Probably an hour or so."

"Okay," he said. "I have food up here for you. Chili and cornbread."

"Sounds amazing," she said, making the turn into the gas

station. She didn't get out of the car after pulling up to a pump. "Anything you need at the grocery store?"

"Doughnuts," he said. "I've been craving a good doughnut."

She giggled, because that was so Theo. He loved baked goods, and Sorrell had put flour, sugar, and baking soda on her grocery list—right at the top.

"Apple fritter?" she asked.

"Always," he said. "And one of those chocolate ones with the cream inside."

"Bavarian," she said. "I have a recipe for those."

"You've teased me with that for years," he said, plenty of flirtation in his tone.

"I never had time," she said, thinking through the next few days. Then a week. Two weeks.

She'd have plenty of time now.

"I also need another gallon of milk," he said. "To go with the doughnuts."

She smiled and shook her head. "You got it, Theo. I'm at the gas station."

"Okay, I'll let you go."

"Bye." Sorrell didn't reach to end the call, though, and it took Theo a few seconds as well.

She sat in her car, a sigh pulling through her. It was made of happiness, but a measure of worry came with it. She sure did like Theo, and while this week apart had been hard and long, it hadn't been anything like the previous two months where she hadn't heard from him at all.

That had been torture.

She did worry about staying in the cabin with him. They had rules, though, and Sorrell reminded herself of that as she got out and started to fill her gas tank.

Everything will be fine, she told herself. *It's Theo, not a blind date.*

At the same time, Sorrell felt like she was skating out onto weak ice. Perhaps because she'd already messed up so badly with Theo. She wanted everything to be perfect between them, or else the ice beneath her feet would crack and break, and she'd fall into frigid water without the hope of a rescue.

Theo would leave the cabin.

They'd break up.

She'd have to start the mourning process all over again, and go through two more months of agony—and maybe more.

Her chest pressed inward, but at least tears didn't show up. She'd been working hard over the past week to tame her emotions. She didn't want them to disappear completely, because she did rely on them in some situations. She simply didn't want to be ruled by them anymore.

It was normal to cry as she hugged her sisters good-bye. They wouldn't be spending the holidays together for the first time ever, and that had struck Sorrell right between the ribs. It was fine to cry about that.

It was not fine to cry about an amazing opportunity to spend time with Theo in a way neither of them had done before. She pressed against that, telling herself she was grateful for his invitation and excited to see him and the cabin. She was even eager to meet his beagles. The way he talked about them, they were dipped in gold and sent straight from heaven.

Sorrell didn't love dogs the way some other people did. Serendipity did though, and she spent as much time looking at the photos Theo had sent as Sorrell did. "He's so lucky," she'd said.

"You should just get a dog if you want one," Sorrell had told her. "Seth Johnson has a ton of them, Seren. Just go get one."

"I'm actually thinking about it," Seren had said, and Sorrell wouldn't be surprised if, when she returned to Chestnut Springs, Seren had a puppy living in the farmhouse.

She'd even texted Brian on her way out of town. *I'm not sure what you're getting Seren for Christmas, but I know she wants a dog.*

Brian probably knew that too, but he'd responded with, *That's a great idea, Sorrell. Drive safe!*

She had driven safe. With her car filled up, she went to the grocery store and bought everything on her list, plus a few extra things to make Bavarian doughnuts from scratch. She bought Theo's requested treats and set the address for the cabin in her navigation program on her phone.

Thirty minutes later, she pulled up to the most beautiful mountain home she'd ever laid eyes on. The windows stretched up and up, and she could only imagine sitting in that loft, reading as the sun brightened another day.

Theo came out onto the deck, three little dogs following

him, and a smile exploded onto Sorrell's face. Theo grinned too, turned, and came down the steps a few seconds later.

She got out of the car, leaving everything behind, and hurried toward him. They were both laughing as he swept her into his arms, and Sorrell almost had an out-of-body experience.

She could see the scene from the outside, as if she were watching it in a movie. She'd seen situations exactly like this in romantic comedies, and she'd never really believed they happened to real people, in real life.

She stood in Theo's arms, though, felt the warmth from his body, and breathed in the piney, woodsy, earthy scent of his skin.

"I thought you'd never get here," he whispered. "I'm so glad you came." He touched his forehead to hers while one of the puppies whined at their feet. "Okay, guys," he said to them, pulling back. "Let's meet the second-in-command." He bent and picked up two of the dogs.

One of them immediately tried to get to Sorrell, and she giggled as she took him from Theo. "This must be Pepper." She grinned at him and then Theo.

"That's right," he said. "He sometimes thinks he's the pack leader, so we have to keep an eye on him." He stooped and picked up the remaining dog. They were so adorable with their long, silky ears and sweet, puppy-dog eyes.

"This is Scout. He won't give you an ounce of trouble. When you want one of them to lay by you, he's your pup." He grinned at the little dog in his arms. "He'd rather be right on top of you, but he'll settle for by your side." He looked at

the last one, a bit wiggly but content in his arms while
Pepper kept lunging at Sorrell's face to try to get a taste of it.

"This is Copper. He keeps the others in line, plus he's
got more brown than the others."

"Oh, I see that," she said. All the puppies looked
different enough to tell them apart instantly, and Sorrell
couldn't help smiling at Theo. "I'm so glad I'm here."

A hint of surprise entered his eyes, further reinforced
when he asked, "Yeah?"

"Yeah," she said, feeling so much and having no way to
articulate it. Perhaps that was her problem. She felt so much
and couldn't express it properly. So it just built up and built
up until she felt like crying.

"Maybe you don't need me for company now that you
have these three," she said, finally bending to put the
rambunctious beagle on the ground.

"Nonsense," Theo said, setting down his two puppies
too. He drew her right against his chest and leaned down.
He didn't ask permission, because he didn't need to. He
kissed her, and Sorrell's dreams once again came true. She
once again imagined herself inside the most romantic movie
in the world, and she'd somehow figured out how to lasso
the sexy, kind cowboy with a heart of gold.

Her stomach growled, and Theo pulled away chuckling.
"Let's get your stuff inside, and then we'll eat. Everything's
ready."

Sorrell laughed too, though even if she wasn't starving,
they couldn't stand around in this cold, kissing.

She gave him a shy glance, glad when she got one in

return, and together, they made several trips to take in her groceries and luggage.

Sorrell took a few extra minutes in the master suite on the top floor, where she'd be living for the next five weeks. It was a huge room, with a dresser, a television on top of that, and almost a whole wall of windows. She had a master closet and a bathroom, all behind one door she could lock. She didn't need to be worried about Theo, she knew that.

Honestly, Sorrell didn't know why she was worried at all. She smoothed down her sweater and went out onto the loft. She couldn't see into the kitchen without leaning over, but she could hear Theo working in there. Bowls clinked together, and the scent of the spicy chili mixed with the newer smell of hot coffee.

All three beagles had curled into one cushion on the couch, and they looked up at her as she gazed down at them. Happiness drew through her, and Sorrell went downstairs to find that tall, broad-shouldered man who'd helped her so often in the kitchen at the farmhouse pulling a bag of shredded cheese from the fridge.

"There you are," he said, looking up at her. "I was just beginning to wonder if you were really going to come down."

"Just checking things out," she said, approaching the counter and taking one of the barstools. She'd always been on the other side of the counter, serving people. She could definitely get used to Theo making dinner for her.

"This is one of those freezer meals I bought," he said. "Remember I texted you about it?"

"Yeah," she said. "Premade, and all you do is heat it up."

"I've had a couple," he said. "They've been pretty good."

"It smells good."

"If it's sick, I have frozen pizza."

"I'm sure it won't be sick." Sorrell smiled at him, finally realizing that *he* was nervous.

He nodded and turned to pick up the slow cooker. He set it on the counter by the bowls, spoons, cheese, and cornbread—which he'd made from a box, he'd said—and looked back at Sorrell.

She didn't hesitate as she stood and joined him in the kitchen, reaching for a bowl as easily as breathing. "What have you been doing this week?"

"Training the dogs," he said. "Resting. Watching TV. Texting you."

"That's it?"

"The dogs are a full-time job," he said, following her as she moved out of the way, her bowl full of chili and cheese now.

"Relaxing sounds nice," Sorrell said, re-taking her barstool. "Last week nearly killed me."

"The bachelor auction," he said. "How'd it go?" He joined her at the bar, and just like that, they slid into their old friendship. He'd always been very easy to talk to, and Sorrell had relied on him so often as a sounding board. She'd told him everything about work—everything that concerned her—and she'd missed that so much after he'd left the ranch.

She detailed her week, ending with, "I'll still have my job when we go back. So that's good. But I'm really looking

Scout returned first, followed by Copper, whose tail stood straight up as it wagged back and forth. He was obviously happier, and Theo scooped them both into his arms as he searched the darkness for the last puppy.

Pepper didn't come, and Theo turned back to the house.

He kept a towel on a hook next to the door, and he'd get these two dried off and cleaned up and come back for Pepper.

Shifting the pups, he managed to get them both supported with one hand and arm so he could reach for the doorknob.

It didn't turn.

Theo's heart sank right down to the soles of his boots and immediately shot back into his chest. His head swam for a moment.

He moved the dogs again and re-gripped the ice-cold metal of the doorknob. It was just finnicky, that was all.

He hadn't locked himself out.

He tried twisting the knob again, but he got the same result. He rattled it back and forth, and in that moment, he had to admit he'd locked himself and the puppies out of the cabin.

He hadn't brought his phone with him, nor his truck keys. He had no idea what time it was or how close dawn was. It didn't matter. He wouldn't last out here for very long, even in the coat and boots.

With his heart pounding, he turned and searched the darkness for Pepper again. He whistled one more time, and added, "Pepper, come on."

The faint sound of jangling came through the midnight stillness of the night, and Theo picked up the little dog and put him with the other two.

"Okay, guys," he said, looking up at the deck above. "We need to figure out how to wake up Sorrell." There wasn't an entrance on the third floor. His only option was to go up the steps to the deck and try the door that led into the living room and kitchen. He had no idea how she slept. Door closed? Open? Earplugs? Music playing? White noise?

In the twenty seconds that it took for him to climb the steps and arrive on the deck, he conjured up a dozen different scenarios of what might happen.

Most of them ended with him and the puppies frozen together as they huddled against this door, waiting and praying for Sorrell to open it.

It was her first night in the cabin; maybe she wouldn't be sleeping well. Or maybe she'd be so tired from all the driving that she'd be out like the dead. Maybe she'd taken a sleeping pill.

Theo's mind would not stop, and he really needed it to. At the same time, he couldn't help thinking, *What would you do if she wasn't here?*

Until last night, she hadn't been. If he'd gotten locked out two nights ago instead of tonight, what would he do?

The cabins up in these mountains weren't so far apart that he couldn't walk to a neighbor's and get help. If there was anyone there, as Theo knew these cabins were second homes or vacation homes. They could be completely unoccupied.

"All right, guys," he said, setting the puppies on the deck. "Stay here, okay?" He faced the door and drew in a deep breath. "Please hear me, Sorrell," he whispered.

He raised both hands and banged on the door, the noise scaring one of the puppies to the point of a yip.

"Sorry," he muttered, suddenly hoping one of the neighbors didn't call the cops. Wait. Yes, they could call the police. That would be fine by Theo. Then maybe he'd be able to get back inside where it was warm.

"Sorrell!" he yelled. "It's Theo. I got locked out." He pounded again, both fists against the wooden door. It sounded like the god of thunder had arrived on the deck, and a healthy dose of embarrassment ran through Theo.

Surely she'd hear that.

He hit the door five, six, seven more times before he stopped. His palms stung, and he looked down at his hands. His gaze went further, and he saw the puppies huddled together, the three of them looking at him like he'd lost his mind.

"We can't stay out here," he said. "We'll all freeze." He waited a few seconds, thinking Sorrell would need a minute to get downstairs and unlock the door.

She didn't come, and Theo repeated the banging, the yelling, the reassurances to himself and the puppies.

Over and over, he tried to wake Sorrell so he wouldn't die on the deck of a cabin he didn't own. Theo thought about the money he had in the bank. The investments he checked so religiously. He saw his whole life right there in front of him, and it wasn't that impressive.

It wasn't impressive at all.

What had he done? How had he helped or influenced anyone? What legacy had he left?

He knew right then and there that he did not want to be like his biological father, alone and bitter at the end of this life. Someone whose children would not even come say good-bye, because they'd done that many years before. They'd parted ways and not looked back.

His teeth started to chatter, and Theo stuck his hands in his pockets and hunched into his coat. He was only wearing basketball shorts, which was fine for a two-minute bathroom break.

He wasn't sure how long it had been since he'd come outside. Or how long since he'd pounded on the door.

"One more time," he told himself, a fierce determination filling him. He wasn't going to give up right here at the entrance. If she didn't come in the next few minutes, Theo would start kicking at the door. He wasn't a small man by any means, and he was getting inside this cabin one way or another.

He hoped it wouldn't be in handcuffs or with his last dying breath, but he'd do what it took.

"Sorrell!" he yelled again, so loud and so long his voice ached. "It's Theo. We got locked out."

He pounded on the door until he couldn't hit it another time. His energy failed him, and such a keen sense of desperation overcame him that he fell to his knees.

"Lord," he said automatically. His voice wavered, and he wasn't sure if that was because his jaw was shaking again or from the complete helplessness filling him. "I need help. Please, wake her up. I can't wake her up." He rested his forehead against the unyielding door, the chill from it seeping right into his skin and skull.

"Please wake her up. I know Thou can wake her up. I can't wake her up." Theo hated this feeling of failure springing up inside him. It watered all the doubts and insecurities he'd ever had, and that kept Theo on his knees.

His eyes burned, and he closed them. One of the puppies whined, and another licked his bare knee. He flinched away from the dog at the same time he heard the most wonderful sound in the world—that of a lock turning.

"Sorrell," he said. "It's Theo. I got locked out."

Before he could stand, the door opened, and Sorrell stood there, holding a piece of wood that should've been used to build a fire. She wielded it like a baseball bat, her eyes wide and afraid.

"It's Theo," he said, scrambling to his feet. "We got locked out when one of the dogs needed to go to the bathroom."

She lowered the log, relief filling her expression now. "Theo," she breathed.

The warmth leaked out of the cabin, and Theo didn't waste another second before reaching for the puppies and stepping inside. All of his muscles trembled, and he glanced at the clock on the microwave.

Just after four in the morning. He still didn't know how long he'd been outside.

"I'm sorry," he said, dropping the puppies. "I've taken

them out at night lots of times. I've never locked myself out." He faced her, his lower jaw still shaking.

"You're freezing," she said.

"A little," he said.

"How long were you out there?"

"I don't know."

"How do we warm you up?" She started looking around like the answer might be in the binder the hosts had left. "I'll get a fire going. You go get in the hot shower."

"I'm—a"

"Now," Sorrell said, pointing down the hall toward the main floor bathroom. "You need to get warmed up quickly. Don't make it too hot, okay? But go."

Theo's mind wasn't really working too great, and he didn't want to argue with Sorrell. He'd already awakened her in the middle of the night. "Sorry," he mumbled again, and he slinked down the hall to the bathroom.

He got the hot water running before he shed his coat and clothes. By then, the steam filled the bathroom, and Theo breathed it in.

Gratitude filled him over and over until it was running out of him. "Thank you," he said over and over as he stepped into the shower. "Thank you, thank you, thank you."

CHAPTER 12

Sorrell hurried around the main level, first getting the fire they'd enjoyed last night going again. With that flickering and crackling, she went into the kitchen to make a pot of coffee. With that percolating, she opened the linen closet and took out two woolly throw blankets. She put them in the dryer on the hottest setting and hurried back upstairs. In her experience, cowboys didn't shower for a terribly long time.

Theo still hadn't come out of the bathroom, though, and Sorrell stood at the mouth of the hallway, worrying over what to do.

What if he wasn't okay in there? What if he'd passed out?

Without another moment of hesitation, she strode down the hall and knocked on the door. Her heartbeat hadn't settled since she'd heard someone banging on the door. She'd held very still in her bed, the covers all the way to her chin, for several minutes. She'd thought perhaps it was just an animal outside. Her mind had taken several paths, none of them good.

She'd finally crept to her bedroom door and opened it. That was when she'd heard Theo's voice. She'd flown into action then, hurrying to put on shoes and a sweatshirt to cover her pajamas. Just to be safe, she'd grabbed a piece of wood from the pile at the bottom of the steps as she'd passed.

She hadn't expected to see Theo on his knees. Her heart tore a little bit for him as she leaned into the bathroom door and knocked. "Theo? Are you okay in there?"

"Yeah," he said, and he sounded exhausted. Sorrell was, she knew that. It had taken her a long time to fall asleep, because she'd been stewing over the man on the other side of this door. He'd been two floors below her, and yes, he'd lived on the same land as her for years. This felt different to her for some reason.

"Okay," she said. "I have warm blankets and hot coffee out here. Do you want me to bring up some different clothes?" He hadn't seemed wet to her, but she thought she'd like to dress in something different than the clothes she'd thought she'd freeze to death in.

"I can get them," he said, his voice moving from muffled in the bathroom to live and in-person as he opened the door. He stood in front of her, a towel wrapped around his waist and one draped over his shoulder.

Most of his torso was completely bare, and his hair shone with dampness.

He was easily the sexiest man on the planet, and Sorrell could only stare at him as he edged out into the hall with her. "I'll be right back," he said.

"Uh huh," Sorrell said, twisting to watch him walk away. He went down the stairs about the time Sorrell got her wits back.

"I put blankets in the dryer down there," she called after him. "Grab them, would you?'

"Yeah," he said, his voice filtering back to her from below. He'd definitely regained some of his confidence, but Sorrell could still see him scrambling to his feet with blue lips and frozen fingers. The relief coming from him had been palpable and not something Sorrell would forget very soon.

"All right." She turned in a full circle, trying to remember where she was and what she'd been doing.

Copper came trotting over to her, and she bent to pick up the puppy. "Hey, you." She kept him tucked under her arm as she got down a couple of coffee mugs from the cupboard. She poured herself a cup of coffee and spooned in plenty of sugar before she heard footsteps behind her.

She turned and stuck the spoon in her mouth as Theo emerged from the basement, both blankets in his hands.

"These are straight from heaven," he said with a smile.

Sorrell twisted to pick up her coffee and handed it to him. "Go sit in front of the fire."

"I'm really okay," he said.

"Go on anyway," she said, hoping she sounded like the strong Texas woman she wanted to be. To her surprise, Theo nodded and ducked his head.

"Yes, ma'am," he said, taking the coffee from her and crossing the room to the hearth. He sat right on the stone and set his coffee down so he could drape one of the blankets around his shoulders.

Sorrell wanted to cuddle with him so badly, but she knew the rock fireplace wouldn't be cuddling-approved. She poured herself a cup of coffee and added sugar and cream before joining him.

He put the second blanket over both of their legs and looked at her. "Thank you for taking care of me. I wasn't thinking super straight there for a bit."

"That's because you were almost frozen." She lifted her coffee cup to her lips. "You scared me though. I heard you for at least ten minutes before I came down." Guilt ripped through her, but Sorrell couldn't rewind time and jump to her feet the moment she'd woken up.

"I'm sorry," he said. "If you hadn't come that last time, I was going to try kicking down the door."

"I'm glad you didn't have to," she said. "Because then we would've had to fix that." She'd also know it was possible, and she'd rather not think about someone less friendly than Theo kicking down the door to the cabin while she slept inside it.

He smiled at her. "I'll take my phone and keys outside with me from now on," he said. "And double-check the locks."

Sorrell grinned back at him, a sense of wooziness and comfort finally replacing the rapid heartbeat in her chest.

She leaned against him, and he lifted his arm up and around her shoulders.

"What were you thinking out there?" she asked.

"At first, I was thinking of what I could do if you didn't let me in. Walk to a neighbor's and hope someone was there. That kind of thing."

Sorrell nodded. She had no idea what she would do if the situation had been reversed. She didn't have the strength Theo did. Her hands weren't nearly as big. Would he have heard her?

The basement door was much closer to his bedroom than the main door had been to hers, so he might hear her.

"Then I realized as I faced the door, my hands stinging and my chest burning, that my life has been pretty meaningless." His voice dropped to almost a whisper, and Sorrell straightened to look at him. "I have a ton of money. I inherited it from my biological father and I've tripled it twice in the stock market. I check my investments about ten times a day. I sell ruthlessly and take big risks on buying."

He looked at her, those deep, dark eyes so wide and vulnerable. "And I realized that none of that matters. Absolutely none of it. I could've frozen to death out there, and no one would care about my investments. No one even knows about them."

"I do," Sorrell said.

"I have a will," he said. "You should know that too. A living trust and will."

"I should probably do that," she said. "Problem is, I don't have anything to put in it." She gave a light laugh, because as much as Theo thought his life was meaningless, Sorrell suspected hers was even more pathetic.

"I need to update mine," Theo said. "Right now, if I get injured, my mother gets to make my medical decisions."

"You don't want her to?"

"My mother is amazing," Theo said. "But no, I don't think she'd even know what to do. I need someone who probably won't die before me."

"I haven't even thought about it," Sorrell said.

"You'd just put one of your sisters there," Theo said. "They can make decisions for you, that kind of thing." His arm around her tightened. "I can help you with it, if you want. I have a great lawyer who set mine up."

"Okay," Sorrell said.

He drew in a deep breath, and several seconds of silence passed. "I realized that I didn't have a legacy, and that I didn't want to die alone, old and bitter, the way my dad did."

Sorrell didn't know what to say to that. She hadn't known his father, and she didn't want to sound like she was passing judgment on the man.

"I want a family," he said quietly. "A lot of kids, who'll come to sit with me when I'm sick. Someone to get me warm blankets and make me take a hot shower, even when I don't want to." He pressed his lips to her temple, and Sorrell's whole world expanded in front of her. "I want to fix the things I do wrong, so there's no bitterness at the end. I want to be surrounded by the people I love, and I want them to *want* to be with me to tell me its okay to let go." He stopped abruptly, and Sorrell didn't dare look at him.

Her own tears had already wetted her eyes, and she knew if she turned her head to look into his, she'd cry. "That sounds nice," she said instead. "I want all of that too."

"Kids, and a husband, and all the warm blankets?"

"Yes," she said with a smile, though she was still battling the tears. "You shouldn't forget about these puppies either." She stretched down to pick up Scout, who'd come over looking for someone to hold him. She handed him to Theo and picked up Copper and then Pepper, who whined and tried to lick her face.

"You get the naughty one," she said, hoping to make the moment lighter.

It worked, because Theo chuckled as he took Pepper off her hands. He said, "Me and Pepper get along so great, because we're so much alike."

"Naughty?"

"A little," Theo said, laughing again. "A little too vocal. We both think we're more important than we are."

Sorrell had enough control of her emotions now to look at him. "You're important, Theo."

He met her eye, and everything turned serious again. Her eyes dropped to his mouth, her fantasies running wild.

"Too vocal and a little naughty," he whispered. "But important."

"That's about right," she said, smiling. She wanted to kiss him again, but something about this moment felt too intimate. She turned away and stroked Copper while Pepper tried to get back to her lap.

Theo murmured to him, and the puppy finally stopped trying.

"You're good with the dogs," Sorrell said.

He took her hand and squeezed it, and Sorrell squeezed back. She should go back to bed, but she was so comfortable and so warm right here beside Theo. She wanted this moment to continue, so she didn't move.

By the time Sorrell came downstairs later, the sun shone fully through those magnificent front windows. Theo had obviously been in the kitchen, because the evidence of lunch sat on the counter. He wasn't there now, though, and Sorrell glanced down the hallway toward the bathroom. The door was open, so he must not be down there either. All three puppies were likewise absent, and Sorrell hummed to herself as she started cleaning up the remains of his sandwich-making.

She wasn't terribly hungry, though she felt like she should be. She pulled a protein shake from the fridge and when she closed it, she found a note stuck to the door.

"Ran to town for a minute," she read out loud. "Call me if you want anything. Should be back by three-thirty."

Sorrell checked the time, and it was quarter to three. He hadn't started back up the canyon to the cabin community.

She couldn't think of a single thing she needed, but she did have one want...

She dialed Theo and when he picked up with a hearty, "There you are. I was just thinking I should've checked to make sure you were alive before I left."

She giggled and shook her head. She'd been abnormally tired after their situation that morning. Deep down, Sorrell knew her exhaustion stemmed from more than that.

Before that Thursday night at the hotel in Austin, she'd been carrying a massive burden. She'd missed Theo with the force of gravity, and she'd been trying to hide how Serendipity's engagement affected her. She worked like a dog at the community center, and she told herself she liked it.

The truth was, she didn't.

She didn't want to work sixty hours a week. She didn't want to hide how she felt about living in the farmhouse alone. She didn't want to live alone at all. She didn't want to think about Theo constantly and not be able to do anything about their situation.

Seeing him at that hostess station had changed everything, and Sorrell still couldn't believe she stood in this cabin at all.

"Sorrell?" Theo asked.

"Sorry." She shook her head to clear it. "Where are you?"

"Getting coffee at one of those drive-through places. Did you want some?"

"No, I'm fine with what we have here."

"Anything else you need?"

"It's not really a need," she said, toeing the ground.

Theo chuckled. "We can get wants too, Sorrell."

"Yeah?" She looked up and out the windows, deciding to walk over to them. "It's almost like we're camping up here, right?"

Theo laughed fully then, and Sorrell liked the sound of it so much. "No, sweetheart. We're not even close to camping."

"Feels like it," she said. "Anyway, I was thinking we needed some s'mores."

"I can hit the grocery store again," he said.

"Great," Sorrell said. "While you're there, see if you can get cinnamon chips. I can make an amazing cinnamon swirl bread for French toast in the morning."

Theo moaned and said, "My mouth is watering already, sugar."

She laughed lightly and a moment later, the call ended. She let her hand holding her phone fall to her side as she continued to gaze out the windows.

Sweetheart. Sugar.

He'd called her both, and Sorrell sure did like how they sounded in his Southern drawl. There wasn't anything she didn't like about Theo, and for the first time in a long time, that fact didn't scare her to death.

What it said, she wasn't sure. She didn't know what step to take next. She hadn't had a boyfriend for a while.

When Theo returned to the cabin, Sorrell got up to help him with the groceries he'd bought. The three pups came in with him, and Sorrell met his eyes. "Hey."

He grinned at her and set down the three paper bags he'd

been carrying. "Hey. There's only a couple more. You don't need to come out." He turned to leave again, and Sorrell hurried after him.

"Theo?"

"Yeah?" He twisted back to her, almost running into her.

She reached up and ran her fingers up the side of his face, the feel of his beard there soft and spiky at the same time. "I—"

Before she could finish, Theo wrapped her in his arms and kissed her. She breathed in through her nose as fireworks popped through her bloodstream. This was the kiss she'd wanted last night but had been too afraid to take.

Theo slowed down instead of speeding up, and Sorrell had never felt as cherished as she did in that moment, and she knew her life would never be the same again.

CHAPTER 13

Theo should stop kissing Sorrell, but he couldn't make himself. She didn't stop either, and he sure did like the way she cradled his face in her hands like she needed him to breathe. She moved her hands into his hair, and sparks raced down his spine.

He liked her too much, he knew. It was the first full day of her stay with him in the cabin, and they weren't married. He couldn't help the naughty paths his mind went down, spurred on by the passion he detected in Sorrell's kiss.

He finally had the bravery to break the kiss, but he couldn't keep his lips to himself. He trailed them down Sorrell's neck, the skin there sweet and delicate. He wanted to taste all of her, right now. Forget about the groceries. Forget that he'd bought ice cream that needed to go in the freezer.

"Theo," she whispered, and Theo drew in a breath and

opened his eyes. Everything swam in his vision, as if Sorrell made him high. In so many ways, she did.

"Sorry," he murmured. "I'll be back in a second." He stepped outside, grateful for the cold now in a way he'd never thought possible after last night. "Get yourself together," he lectured himself as he went down the steps. "She's not going to sleep with you. Not now. Not tonight. Not at all—not until you marry her."

Theo gathered the last two bags of groceries, as well as the real reason he'd made the drive down the canyon—the WiFi router that would allow him to use his streaming television services up here—and headed back to the cabin.

Sorrell stood with her back to him, putting something in the fridge. He'd always admired her, and guilt gutted him. He set the other bags heavily on the counter and said, "Sorrell, I'm sorry about that kiss."

She turned toward him. "You are? Why?"

He blinked at her. "You didn't think it was inappropriate?"

She reached up and tucked her hair behind her ear. He sure did like this makeup-less version of the woman, even if he'd seen her before. She seemed so casual right now, and he liked that she was comfortable enough around him to just be herself.

"I don't know," she said, refusing to look at him as she simply started unpacking another bag of food.

"My—uh—I started thinking inappropriate things," he said. "I shouldn't kiss you like that." He put both hands on the countertop and leaned into it, waiting for her to look at him. "Sorrell."

She finally glanced up, and it was as if time paused again. Theo's mind misfired, and he wondered what in the world he'd been thinking when he invited her up here to skip Christmas with him.

"I won't do it again, okay?" He raised his eyebrows. He needed her to understand what she did to him. "I like you a whole lot, Sorrell. Just because I left the ranch doesn't mean that changed."

"Okay," she said. "I like you too, Theo."

"Okay," he said.

She abandoned the groceries and rounded the peninsula to stand in front of him. "What if I liked how you kissed me?"

"Doesn't matter," he said, resisting the urge to draw her against his chest again. "It's not...we're not married, and I... men are different than women, Sorrell." He allowed himself to look into her eyes. "Don't worry, okay? My hormones will settle down, and it won't be a problem."

"Can I still kiss you?"

Theo grinned at her, letting himself reach out with one hand. He brushed her arm with his fingertips and nothing more. "Yeah, I'll still let you kiss me, sugar."

She inched closer to him until he had no choice but to put his arms around her. "But not like that," he whispered into her hair. "Okay? If we're going to live here together for the next five weeks, I have to have boundaries for myself. I crossed it already, and I'm sorry."

"Okay," she said, holding him as tightly as he held her. Theo's eyes drifted closed, and he reveled in the feeling of being adored by such a good woman.

"Okay," he said, stepping back. "Now, I think you said something about s'mores."

"You don't want dinner first?"

"We're adults, sweetheart. I can eat dessert before dinner if I want to." He picked up a package of marshmallows. "And tonight, I want to."

"You can just let me out here," Sorrell said, glancing out her window.

"I can take you to the corner," Theo said, his tone on the outer edge of annoyed. He was sure Sorrell heard it, especially because she glanced at him.

Her eyes hooked into the side of his face. "I said I could drive myself."

"It snowed ten inches overnight," Theo said. "Your sedan wouldn't have made it out of the driveway." He cut a look at her too. "It's fine, Sorrell. I'm fine."

She folded her arms and glared out the windshield. "Theo," she said, a forced measure of calm in her voice. Theo knew, because they'd spent plenty of time together over the past two weeks. Hours and hours every day.

"What?" he asked when she didn't continue.

"I know you're not fine when you use my name," she

said. "So stop lying to me and just let me out here. I can walk the rest of the way."

"Sorrell, I—"

"Let me out now," she said, and Theo knew better than to argue with her when she spoke in that tone.

"Okay, don't get out while we're still moving." He put on his blinker and pulled to the side of the street.

Sorrell exhaled in a long, steady stream and looked at him. She put a bright smile on her face. "Thank you, Theo. I'm sure I'll be done before your movie is over." She reached for the door handle and spilled from his truck to the curb in the next moment.

"Call me if you need more time," he called after her.

She said, "I will," and closed the door. She stepped through the snow and slush to the cleared sidewalk and started down the street without ever looking back at him.

He wasn't worried about her in Beaver Creek alone. It was a quaint town, with plenty of mountain charm and good people. He'd taken Scout, Pepper, and Copper to see their original owners twice now, and there was always someone to help him find something at the grocery store he'd never heard of before.

Sorrell had been true to her word, and she'd cooked for them almost every day. To do that, she needed ingredients, and that meant Theo always had quite the exotic list for the grocer in town.

He eased back into traffic and turned left to get away from Main Street. The town loved its holiday decorations, and with only three days until The Big Day, everything on

Main Street was decked out in pine boughs, red bows, and tinsel.

Theo never went there, and he hadn't bought a single gift for anyone this year, not even his mother. He'd spoken to her plenty of times—a couple of those with Sorrell on speakerphone with him. His mother asked embarrassing questions, and after the conversation where she'd asked Theo if he was sleeping with Sorrell, he'd taken their conversations back into private.

Of course he and Sorrell weren't being intimate. He hadn't allowed himself to kiss her so passionately again. He'd kept his thoughts on appropriate paths as he and Sorrell talked, as they watched movies, as they held hands and snuggled and yes, kissed.

He was a grown man, and he could control his hormones, something he'd been very blunt about with his mother. In that same conversation, he'd reminded her he was skipping Christmas and asked her to please not send him anything. He wouldn't be sending her anything either.

She'd agreed, but as Theo put more distance between himself and Main Street, the only thing he could feel was guilt.

Sorrell had been planning this trip to town to pick up a few things for her sisters for a week. It wasn't her fault the snow had started yesterday afternoon and hadn't stopped until dawn. He'd said he'd drive her, and he had. He could go to a movie while she shopped. It wasn't a big deal.

It really wasn't, but Theo regretted being beastly to her about it.

He stopped at a red light and pulled his phone from the console. *Sorry I was short with you.*

He sent the text as the light turned green, and he dropped the phone back in the cupholder so he could drive properly. To his right, a sign caught his attention.

A ring for any occasion.

Before he knew it, he had his blinker on again and he was turning into the parking lot of the jewelry store. Only a couple of cars sat there, and Theo peered through the windshield at the glass and stone building. It looked newer than a lot of the other buildings Theo had seen around town.

He got out, not sure what he was planning to do. Inside, a blast of heat relaxed him, as did the woman smiling her way toward him. "Good afternoon," she said. "My name is Rosanne. Is there something I can help you find?"

Theo hooked his thumb over his shoulder. "That signs says a ring for any occasion. I guess I want to see those kind of rings."

The jewelry cases spread before him, and there were so many, Theo thought sure some of them would have to be empty. No store had that many rings.

Turned out, this one did. Rosanne turned and talked over her shoulder. "What kind of occasion are you looking for? Something for Christmas?"

"No," he practically barked.

"Birthday? For your mother? Girlfriend? Sister?" Rosanne didn't seem fazed by his attitude.

"Girlfriend," he said, though he was now considering a ring for his mother too. "There's no real occasion. Just maybe something to say, this is from me?" Foolishness streamed through him.

"I've got something like that," she said, leading him past several of the front cases. Most of them looked like they held diamonds and only diamonds. Theo had started to fall for Sorrell, that was for sure. He'd been falling for her for seven years. He still didn't think they were to diamond level yet.

"These are some of our more unique stones," Rosanne said. "They're sourced locally or here in the West, and they're more about reminding someone of an experience than saying anything like *I love you* or *marry me*." She smiled with perfect precision, and Theo returned the gesture before looking into the case.

He didn't recognize any of the stones except the turquoise, but he did like what he was seeing. "Not gems," he said. These stones didn't sparkle. They were stones, with beautiful veins of coloration, but opaque. There was every color in the rainbow, and Theo got lost for a moment taking them all in.

"These are beautiful," he said.

"Do you have an idea of what color she'd like?" Rosanne asked.

"She wears a lot of neutral stuff," he said. "For her job." Around the cabin, Sorrell wore loose yoga pants and sweatshirts. Her hair was always clean though, and she always seemed put together despite her lack of pencil skirts, heels, and makeup. She was classy and sophisticated in a Texan sort of way that made his pulse pound no matter how many times he watched her come down the stairs from her bedroom.

"I like the buffalo turquoise," Rosanne said, pulling out a long bar with several rings on it. "It's this black and white one. Every stone is going to be different, due to the striations. Some are more white. Some more black."

Theo examined the rings, all of which held a black and white stone perched on a silver band. Some stones were large, and some small. Some bands sported a bit more ornate design. The choices were endless.

"Do you have a budget in mind?" Rosanne asked. "That sometimes helps narrow things down."

He looked away from the buffalo turquoise and focused on the colored stones. "No budget," he said almost absentmindedly. "I think the buffalo turquoise is nice," he said. "I don't think she's a big ring wearer. So something smaller."

"This one has a nice setting," Rosanne said, indicating one of the smaller pieces. It wasn't perfectly round, which Theo liked, and the silver extended up over the edge of the turquoise in a row of balls that shone.

"White gold?" he asked. "Or silver?"

"White gold," the woman said. "We make all of our rings right here in the shop. The stones and gems are bought and brought in raw. We polish them, design the settings, and set them ourselves."

Theo looked up at her. No wonder there weren't any other customers in here. "You do?"

"The store is owned by Karl Millstone," she said with a

smile. "He purchases all of the stones and gems personally, and his son and daughter are the master jewelry-makers."

Theo liked that, and he returned Rosanne's smile. "That one is kind of brown."

"Every piece is unique," she said without missing a beat. "The buffalo turquoise is one of the most rare forms of turquoise. It comes from a single mine in Nevada. There's nowhere else on earth to get it, and one family mines it."

"What's the most rare form of turquoise?" he asked.

"The Lander blue spiderweb turquoise is extremely rare," Rosanne said. "It also comes from Nevada."

She brought out another bar. "We have only two pieces with the Lander blue."

Theo didn't like them nearly as much. "It's pretty," he said. "But I like this black and white better." He touched a ring that had an oval piece of the buffalo turquoise, with a simple band and a ring of silver around the stone that was smooth and blemish-free.

It was simple but elegant. Sophisticated and beautiful. Stated but not *over*stated.

It spoke to Theo's soul and told him this piece of jewelry was everything Sorrell was too.

"I like that one," he said.

"Do you happen to know her ring size?" Rosanne asked as she slipped the ring off the display.

"No idea," Theo said.

"She can get it sized at any ring shop," Rosanne said. "Our jewelers will do it for free, of course, and if you can find out while you're here in town, we can do it in an hour or so."

He wondered if she ever got tired of smiling. What was she like behind closed doors? Did she dress down into sweatpants and bare feet too?

Theo supposed she did, and he said, "Let me make a phone call." He stepped away and dialed Sorrell, trying to find a reason why he needed to know her ring size.

"Hello, Theodore," she said, and Theo froze to the spot.

"Theodore?" He almost started chuckling, but the ice in his chest made it really hard.

"Yes," she said. "You use my name when you're irritated with me. I'm going to use Theodore when I'm irritated with you."

"You're irritated with me?" he asked.

"Yes," she said simply.

Theo peered down into the nearest ring case, his pulse puttering a little bit now. The last thing he wanted was Sorrell to be upset with him. "What can I do about that?"

"Nothing," she said. "Just let me have my afternoon, and we'll be fine by dinner."

"What's your ring size?" he asked oh-so-casually.

"My ring size? Why do you need to know?"

"Maybe your boyfriend would like to buy you a gift to say he's sorry for whatever he did to make his girlfriend annoyed with him."

Sorrell sighed, and that caused a grin to jump to Theo's face. He was eternally glad she wasn't with him, though, because he didn't think Sorrell would appreciate the fact that he'd broken down her irritation in a couple of sentences.

"Not all situations can be fixed with gifts, you know."

"Oh, come on." Theo laughed, making sure not to let it go on too long. "You think anything can be fixed with food. Gifts are like that for men."

"I do *not* think anything can be fixed with food."

"Carbs then," he teased. "In fact, I distinctly remember you saying carbs could fix anything."

"Maybe you should be getting me a cinnamon roll then," she quipped.

Theo laughed again and said, "Who says I'm not?"

"You really are annoying," she said darkly. "But if you must know, my ring size is a seven."

"I must know," he said. "So thank you, sugar."

"Oh, don't *sugar* me," she said with bite. "You're just as irritated with me right now as I am with you."

Theo didn't want to argue with her. The truth was, his annoyance with her had ended the moment she'd gotten out of the truck. He was going to have to pick her up with all those shopping bags though. They'd probably be red and green, with silver and gold bows. Or decorated with Christmas trees and reindeer.

"Okay," he said. "You're right. I'll see you in a couple of hours."

"Goodbye, Theodore."

He waited to hang up before he chuckled. He turned around. "She's a size seven."

"If you have a few minutes, we can take care of this right

now," Rosanne said. She passed the ring to another man who was equally as well-dressed as she was. "I can check you out right here, and they'll get that polished up and sized for you."

Theo was going to miss his movie, but he decided he didn't care. He did need an afternoon to himself, but it didn't have to be spent in a movie theater.

As he paid and went to his truck to wait for the ring to be cleaned and sized, he prayed. *Please let Sorrell get over her irritation with me.*

He was also glad he now had a gift to give her to apologize. All she needed to see was that someone could give gifts any time of year. It didn't have to be Christmas to do that.

He didn't think she'd see his side of the argument though, and he knew if he wanted to keep Sorrell in his life long-term, he was going to have to figure out how to celebrate Christmas.

CHAPTER 14

Sorrell woke the next morning to the scent of bacon. Maybe sausage. Surprise accompanied the smells, because she and Theo had had a very specific conversation about the meals over the next couple of days.

In her family, they had a huge breakfast on Christmas Eve. He wanted to skip the day completely. She hadn't said he couldn't. She hadn't said she'd go ahead with her family traditions though she wasn't with her family. In the end, they'd simply agreed to allow today to be whatever it was going to be.

Sorrell already knew what kind of perfect storm she'd find in the kitchen. A Theo who cooked was a Theo trying to pound something out from inside him. She supposed she liked to cook and bake for the same reason. It soothed her.

"His biological father died on Christmas Eve," she reminded herself. She could be more sensitive to him today.

He'd picked her up yesterday afternoon with a simple, "Hey."

She'd responded with, "Hey, how was the movie?" as she climbed into the cab.

"I didn't go," he said. That was all. He didn't say why. He didn't say where he had gone. He never presented her with a gift, and she hadn't seen hide nor hair of a gift box, bag, or bow.

She'd stashed her bags in the back seat before getting in the front, trying to conceal them as much as possible from Theo. She really was trying to respect his wishes that they skip Christmas this year. If she were being honest with herself, it was harder to do than Sorrell had anticipated. She'd thought that the isolated environment would make it easier, but it didn't. She wasn't lonely, but she did miss her sisters, and that meant a lot of texting and phone calls. She followed friends and family on social media. She couldn't avoid the pictures of their Christmas meals, their family parties, their gift-wrapping sessions, or their mantles with the stockings all hung with care.

She'd been seeing them all, and over the past week, her heart had started to ache that she wouldn't be participating in anything holiday-related.

By the time she showered and went downstairs, Theo sat at the dining room table with an empty plate in front of him. That wasn't uncommon; they'd been eating together if they were in the kitchen together for breakfast. Lunch was an entirely different affair. Theo called her a "lunchtime diva" because she always wanted something hot for lunch. He liked making sandwiches out of everything.

She made dinner almost every night, and they shared that meal together. But breakfast was open season.

"I made bacon and sausage," he said. "Put it all in an omelet. You want one?"

"Yes, please," she said, pouring herself a cup of coffee. He joined her in the kitchen, and the delicate dance began. She stirred in sugar and side-stepped around him to get the cream.

He wore the storm in his soul like a cape, and Sorrell wanted to rip it off and shake it out. She'd tried to ask him about his father previously, but Theo had said he didn't have anything else to tell her.

As he cracked eggs and started whisking everything together, Sorrell leaned against the counter and asked, "What's on the agenda for today?"

"Just this," Theo said without looking at her.

"Maybe we should take the dogs for a hike."

He poured the omelet into the hot pan, where it hissed. He looked at her as he picked up the rubber spatula. "You hate hiking. Besides, it's called snowshoeing when the hike is buried under twelve feet of snow." He tossed her a grin that barely reached the corners of his mouth.

"I know," she said, her voice pitching up. "I meant *you* should take the dogs for a snowshoeing adventure, and I'll sit in the truck and read." She smiled at his back, hoping the realness of hers would permeate his soul.

He shook his head and chuckled. "They'll be wet when we get back."

"We'll throw some towels in the back seat," she said. "Believe it or not, they don't have to ride up front with us."

"Surely you jest," he said, finally turning around with a genuine smile on his face. "Will you make your mother's homemade mac and cheese for lunch?"

Sorrell calmly lifted her coffee mug to her lips and sipped. After swallowing, she said, "If you want."

"Do we have the stuff?" he asked.

"The only odd thing is brown mustard," she said. "We could stop on the way back from the hike."

Theo didn't commit to anything. He turned back to the stove and folded her omelet in half, sliding it onto a plate in the next few seconds.

"Here you go," he said, putting the plate on the counter beside her. He started to turn away, but Sorrell grabbed his arm.

"Theo," she said, making her voice kind and soft. "Tell me what I did so I can apologize for it. I didn't talk about the shopping at all. I hid the bags. I waited to get them until you were downstairs. I tried, Theo. I really—"

"It's not you," he said.

She searched his face, trying to find the reason for the unrest inside him. "You're not okay."

He gathered her into his arms, and Sorrell wrapped hers around him too, holding him as tightly as she could. "I want to help you."

"You are," he said. "Just being here helps me."

Sorrell didn't want to press him further, so she just stayed within the safe circle of his arms and let him hold her. When he finally released her, he said, "That's going to be cold now."

"It's okay." She picked up the plate and opened the nearby drawer for a fork. "You get the dogs ready to go hiking, and I'll eat, and we'll go."

Theo did as she said, picking up the leashes and letting them jingle so the dogs would know that he was going to take them out. Pepper started to whine, as usual, and he got the other two a little bit riled up, especially Copper. Sorrell cut off a piece of her omelet and held it up, and all three dogs settled right down.

She giggled while Theo shook his head at her, a real smile on his face.

Copper loved to go outside, and Sorrell had learned in the last couple of weeks that he was the rambunctious one that led the others into unknown places. Pepper was the one who stayed in those places and caused the most trouble while there. Scout was afraid of his own shadow most of the time, though he did find a couple of white rabbits out in the snow that he enjoyed chasing around.

"Come on guys," Theo said. "Let's get ready to go. Sorrell says that we can go on a hike today." He clipped the leashes to the dog's collars, and they didn't give him any trouble. He had been taking them on walks and making sure that they got used to leashes, coming back when he whistled, and waiting to eat until he told them they could.

Sorrell watched him do all of those things from the

safety of the covered deck. They'd learned that there were heaters in the ceiling of the deck, and she could sit out there and read while Theo played with the dogs in the yard below.

He'd told her he wanted to be the pack leader in this pack of dogs and all three of them did what he said most of the time. Pepper was the most disobedient, but he still sat when Theo said, and he still waited to get his leash on when Theo told him to do so.

Theo left the dogs behind and loaded up all the snowshoes while Sorrell collected several hand warmers. She got out the dogs' portable water bottles, as well as her tablet and a charger for her phone so she could look at her social media while Theo hiked.

Sorrell hadn't said a single thing while they got everything ready. She wasn't going to say anything now either. Theo had something on his mind, something that was bothering him, but it was up to him to say what it was. She wasn't going to initiate another conversation about his father.

She wasn't sure if she'd want to talk about him. He'd said very little in the past, and he probably just needed this day to be contemplative and relaxing.

If Sorrell's memory was right, his biological father had died years and years ago. But her mother had died a long time ago, too. That pain still sometimes came back and stung her at odd times. She and her sisters had gone out to their father's grave last summer and done a small ceremony with all of them and their significant others.

Sorrell had liked that Theo had been there. Perhaps they

could talk about what it was like to lose somebody and how you carried on after the fact. She took a deep breath, trying to find the right words to say, and then with nothing came, she started a prayer in her heart. She didn't know what to say for that either.

She simply let Theo drive, the radio playing in the background and the three dogs on the seat between them. Thankfully, they weren't very big dogs.

Yet, Sorrell thought, wondering how big they'd really get and if Theo would let them sleep with him if they got too large.

"How long do you think you'll be gone?" she finally asked.

"I don't know," Theo said. "Not long, I suppose. It's still really cold out there."

"True," she said, and the conversation ended. Sorrell had never minded the silence between her and Theo, because they were good friends and they didn't have to talk all the time. She usually liked the comfortable pauses between what they had to say. But today, she was uncomfortable.

It was Christmas Eve, and it just didn't feel right to be acting like it didn't exist. She'd also never known Theo to act like he was okay when he wasn't. She hated that she was pretending like she didn't care that she wasn't at the farmhouse with her sisters, where she'd always been.

She bit her tongue because she'd promised Theo that she could come to this cabin and skip Christmas with him. She'd *promised*, and she *could* do it.

Theo pulled up to a popular place to go snowshoeing,

and there were several other cars there. Apparently, going snowshoeing in the middle of winter was a very popular thing to do in the mountains of Colorado.

Sorrell pulled out her tablet and said, "I'll just wait here."

"Do you want me to leave the truck on?"

"Leave me the keys. It's okay if you turn it off for now. I've had my seat heater going, and I should be fine for a while." She tapped to open her streaming app so she could watch a show. If he really was only going to be gone for a little bit, she'd probably only be able to watch one episode.

Maybe she'd be able to call her sisters to find out what they were doing for the holidays.

Theo got out of the truck and turned back for the dogs. "Come on, guys. Right here by me." The three of them jumped down, and Theo gave her one more smile before he closed the door and headed toward the tailgate.

She watched in the rearview mirror while he strapped on the snowshoes, put on a backpack, put a whistle around his neck, and attached the leashes to a strap that went around his waist from the backpack. He claimed to like snowshoeing, and he'd told her lots of times that she'd probably like it too.

She really didn't want to try snowshoeing. She was more the type of person who liked to stay indoors. She was the one who made the potato salad while everybody went swimming or hiking—or if she lived in a cold climate, sledding. She was the one who'd have hot doughnuts and hot coffee ready for when they got back.

Today, there were no such meals; she would not be making a holiday lunch or dinner for Christmas, though macaroni and cheese was very Texas. She had to be okay with that. Theo had left the keys, but he'd killed the engine, so her phone didn't connect to the Bluetooth when she called Serendipity.

"Sorrell," her sister said. "Merry Christmas." She sounded so happy, and that made Sorrell's emotions soar toward the sky.

"Merry Christmas," Sorrell said, relieved her voice didn't give away the fact that she was missing her sisters more than she'd thought she would.

"What are you up to?" Serendipity asked. "I thought you weren't celebrating Christmas."

"Theo went hiking with the pups. I'm just waiting for him in the truck."

"Waiting for him in the truck?"

"Yes," Sorrell said. "I didn't want him to go alone. It's kind of dangerous to do that out here in the wilderness anyway." Not that she knew what she could do if he got injured or hurt. The man was easily twice as big as her, and there was no way that she could carry him anywhere, or even get him in the truck if he couldn't get in himself.

"What do you do in the truck while you wait?" Serendipity asked.

"Watch TV," Sorrell said. She was a pro at watching TV. It had become her way of unwinding after a long and stressful day of dealing with a lot of people, a lot of meetings, a huge budget, and a deep bureaucracy at the community center in Chestnut Springs.

Sorrell could admit that she did not miss her job. She thought she would, and that was very surprising thing for her. Serendipity loved her job at Enchantment Rock. Sarena loved anything to do with ranching, horses, dogs, cattle, and fields. Now that Sarena had a baby, she did focus more on her family than she did the farm, which was why she'd hired three more cowboys since Theo had left. Sorrell liked them all. It was fine for her to cook meals for them. She didn't mind talking to them. They were all polite and kind when they came to the farmhouse. None of them had been Theo, and she reminded herself that it was a small price to pay to overlook a major holiday so that she could spend time with the man she knew she was steadily falling in love with.

"Sorrell?" Serendipity asked.

"Yeah," Sorrell said. "I'm still here."

"I thought I lost you for a second."

"Are you at the farmhouse by yourself?" she asked Serendipity.

"I'm actually at Brian's," Seren said. "He's making a big turkey dinner for us."

"He is?" Sorrell asked. "I didn't know he could do that."

"Yeah, well I didn't either," Seren said with a light laugh. "He does say he knows how to cook, and he can take care of himself." She paused and then said in a low voice, "Good thing too, because I'm not even sure how to mash potatoes."

Sorrell laughed, because it was true. Serendipity was the youngest sister, and she'd never had to learn how to cook, because Sorrell loved it so much. Sarena had learned from their mother, just as Sorrell had, but she didn't love it. Sorrell had always manned the kitchen at the farmhouse, and she didn't mind cooking for her sisters.

She wondered where she would be if she were back on the ranch right now. Sarena had her own life now in a new house down the lane. And if Seren were out at Brian's, where would Sorrell be?

Alone in the farmhouse, she thought. *That's where you'd be.*

She realized she really wasn't losing anything by being here with Theo. It didn't matter if there wasn't a pine wreath on the door, and it didn't matter that they didn't have a Christmas tree with red and gold balls and white lights and plenty of tinsel.

It didn't matter. They were together, and Sorrell should want that more than she wanted a big festive celebration with red bows and silver bells.

She swallowed her pride and checked her feelings and asked Seren how Sarena was doing with West, and what they were doing for Christmas. She listened while Seren talked, and then Seren said, "Oh, the timer is going off. I have to go, Sorrell."

Sorrell said, "Merry Christmas," one more time and hung up. Her voice choked in her throat, and thankfully she didn't have anything to say to anyone else. She started her television program, but she didn't really watch it. She thought about Theo instead.

All of a sudden, she knew exactly what to pray for, and

that was clarity of mind, and the exact right words to help him through this hard time. It was a good reminder for Sorrell that not everything was about her. Surely Theo knew that skipping Christmas was hard for her. Of course he knew.

They'd already had a little argument yesterday about the shopping. She was trying to spare his feelings. He was trying to make sure that her needs were met.

By the time Theo returned, Sorrell had watched one episode of her crime drama, and she was happy to see him. His face was mostly pink, covered by that sexy beard. He lifted the dogs up into the truck one by one, and they all came over to greet her.

She giggled as they acted like they'd been gone for weeks, and she pushed them back with the words, "No, don't climb on me." They were definitely wet, and she reached into the back seat and grabbed the towel so that she could clean them up. Theo removed his snowshoes and loaded everything into the back of the truck before he got behind the wheel.

"How was your show?" he asked.

"Good," she said. "How was the hike?"

"Good enough," he said as he started the truck.

"Do you...?" She paused. Though she'd prayed for the words to come, she still wasn't sure if they were there. "Do you want to talk about your dad?"

He looked at her. Those dark, beautiful eyes so full of everything in that moment. Theo felt a lot of things, and Sorrell could see them all swirling in his expression. He didn't vocalize even one half of what he thought or felt, and she wished he would.

She couldn't change who he was, though. That was something Sorrell had learned from an old boyfriend. She just wanted to be there for him if he had anything to say.

"You don't have to tell me," she said. "But I'm here for you if you need me."

He reached across Pepper, Scout and Copper, and took her hand in his. "Having you here is everything, sugar."

Sorrell smiled at the endearment, glad he hadn't used her name.

"Thank you for being here. I know it's not easy for you."

"You've actually done me a great favor. I've learned that I don't really like my job. My sisters get along just fine without me." She turned away from him, experiencing some of her own heavy emotions in that moment.

"You don't like your job?" Theo asked. "I've always thought you really enjoyed it."

"Me too," Sorrell said. She didn't know how to explain. Maybe she just liked living in a cabin in the woods, and it sure was nice when she didn't have to think about bills. Somebody else took the trash out, and for the most part, somebody else made breakfast. All Sorrell had to do was read, watch TV, and make dinner. All things that she really enjoyed doing.

"Are you going to quit when you get back?" Theo asked.

"I don't know," Sorrell said. "Honestly, I really am considering it, but I don't know what I would do." She turned her attention back to him, proud of herself that she'd been able to tame her emotions and speak like a normal person. She felt like she was getting a little bit better every day at controlling the tears and letting herself feel something without crying about it.

"Not all of us are independently wealthy," she teased. "I do have to work if I want to pay my bills."

He looked out the windshield as a crash of thunder filled the air. "We better get back," he said. "We don't want to be out in the storm. I'll make sure we have enough wood. We'll put something on the TV that you want to watch."

"Did you still want me to make mac and cheese?" she asked.

He shifted in his seat. "I figure you can make something festive if you want."

Her eyebrows lifted, and she looked at him, but he wouldn't look back at her. "I don't have to do that, Theo."

"My dad loved fried chicken," he said. "I was thinking about him on the hike. Maybe we could have that in honor of him."

"Sure," she said. "I've got the ingredients for mashed potatoes and brown gravy."

Theo let a smile move across his face, and it was the most beautiful thing Sorrell had seen in a long time. She didn't mind the stormy quiet version of Theo quite as much as she thought she would

"Sure," he said. "Fried chicken, mashed potatoes, and brown gravy."

"I'd make collard greens," she said. "But I don't think we

have any of that. In fact, I don't even think you could buy stuff like that in the grocery store here."

Theo chuckled, and he said, "You're probably right," as he put the truck in gear and got them headed back to the cabin.

It was early afternoon by the time they returned, but Sorrell got to work right away on dinner. She'd eat a mid-afternoon meal and be done, and Theo could get leftovers out of the fridge if he was hungry later—and he would be.

He put something on the television in the living room and lay down on the couch. She wasn't sure if he'd fallen asleep or not, but he didn't say anything.

Forty minutes later, she went into the living room and peered over the back of the couch. Sure enough, Theo had fallen asleep.

Watching him sleep, with such peace on his face, Sorrell could admit how much she liked him. She wondered if she'd already fallen in love with him. It felt like it, and it felt good.

"Theo," she whispered, but it wasn't nearly loud enough to wake him.

He'd always been there for her. If she needed a table set up, Theo did it. If she was having a bad day, Theo would bring her a cookie from town. When she struggled after Sarena got married, Theo had come to the farmhouse and stood at the sink and did dishes with her.

It was always Theo. Always right there at her side.

He'd never said the three words *I love you* out loud to her before. As she thought about all of the acts of service, all of the kindness that he had offered her over the years, and combined that with the way he kissed her and the way he'd asked her out over and over, Sorrell realized that the man had been in love with her for a very long time.

Something warmed inside her. It always felt good to feel loved, and she was grateful for that. At the same time, she wondered what he'd been getting back from her.

Rejection after rejection. A weepy woman who couldn't do anything. What did he see in her that spoke to his soul?

She'd made a dinner for him to commemorate his father. She'd suggested the hike that had calmed him. She was skipping Christmas, because he wanted to.

She hoped that she could be the person he needed in his life, and she reached out and trailed her fingers down the side of his face. Her nerves pulsed through her veins, because she wasn't sure if she was scared or excited to think about being that woman for many years to come.

CHAPTER 15

Theo woke on Christmas morning and pushed one of the dogs off his hip so he could roll over. All three pups immediately came toward him, one of them—most likely Pepper—licking his face like it was long past time to get up.

"Stop it," he mumbled to them, because the room was still plenty dark. He didn't need this day to be any longer than it was already going to be. He'd so enjoyed yesterday afternoon. He'd been grouchy—beyond grouchy—in the morning, but the hike Sorrell had suggested had evened everything out for him.

He'd taken a nap while Sorrell made fried chicken and mashed potatoes, and Theo was convinced there wasn't anything the woman couldn't make to absolute perfection. He'd been a bit somber while they ate, but Sorrell talked about her mom and dad, how they'd died, and how much she missed them.

Just that simple conversation in her sweet voice had reminded Theo that he wasn't the only one who'd experienced loss. Sorrell had definitely been through more than him, as she didn't have a mother or a father on the earth anymore. He'd experienced a few minutes of regret then, because he should've known she was going through her own turmoil.

They'd both perked up when she brought out the ice cream, and they'd snuggled together on the couch in front of the fireplace to watch movies that night. The day had definitely ended on a high note, and Theo had dragged himself away from kissing the woman and downstairs to his bedroom.

He'd been on his best behavior over the last few weeks when it came to Sorrell, and sometimes it sure was exhausting. He sighed as he started rubbing the dogs and telling them what good boys they were. They'd stayed beside him on the hike yesterday, none of them even pulling a little bit. He loved that he could take them with him and have them behave, and he knew it was because of his intense training since he'd picked them out of that plastic bin.

They all loved getting rubbed down in the morning, and Theo found the action soothing as well. He was the one who woke early in the mornings, and he made breakfast nine days out of ten. Today, though, he stayed in bed for another half-hour. Then another.

Sorrell would probably just pour herself a bowl of cereal. She claimed not to make breakfast very often, because getting out of the house in the morning was tough enough.

He'd definitely eaten quiches she'd made in the past, so he knew she had some morning recipes up her sleeve.

The woman had a lot up her sleeve. Theo had thought he knew Sorrell pretty well, but he'd learned even more about her by being in the cabin with her. He knew she liked baggy sweatshirts, and she didn't like being cold, and she loved to snack on crackers in the afternoon while she read. He'd never seen someone buy five boxes of wheat thins at once, and she did that every time they went shopping.

She had a little bit of anxiety about running out of things, especially toilet paper. Theo thought they had enough to last whoever came to stay in the cabin for the next year, and a chuckle slipped between his lips.

He'd also realized that Sorrell was much less emotional than he'd originally thought. He'd learned that he spent most of his time around her at the ranch when she was in a situation of high stress. Her sister was moving out. Her father had died. She had an enormous event at work. Anything that piled on top of those stressors leaked out of Sorrell in the form of tears.

He'd never known the woman to simply sit and watch TV. At the ranch, she worked full-time at the community center, or was making dinner, or cleaning up after dinner. She rarely sat down, and Theo had admired her work ethic.

Here, she sat. She read. She took naps. She watched TV with him. She didn't like the snow, so any hiking or walking was out, but she'd come downstairs and played ping pong with him a couple of times too. She really wasn't very good at it, and Theo couldn't help smiling again.

He allowed himself to think through his feelings for Sorrell and really examine them, something he rarely did. He'd been infatuated with her for years. The attraction between them had always felt as strong as gravity, and leaving Fox Hollow Ranch had been terrible. Theo did wonder, though, that if his new ranch had been better, if he'd be where he was right now.

Perhaps he'd still be working at that new ranch and getting to know new friends. Maybe even a new woman.

He didn't think he'd have gotten over Sorrell in only two months. He also wasn't sure if he was in love with her, or just very close to it.

His phone chimed, and Theo groaned as he reached for it. He'd deliberately made sure his alarm was off, though he hadn't really expected that he could sleep much past dawn. The puppies still needed to go out first thing in the morning, and once Theo got out of bed, he didn't get back in. He could nap in the afternoon, and that had helped him stay up late enough to watch movies with Sorrell and kiss her good-night.

He had stopped taking the puppies out in the middle of the night, and he was grateful for that. He sat up and picked up his phone to find his mother had texted. *I'm not sure of the time difference where you are, Theodore. Call me when you get a moment, would you?*

Theo looked up from the phone as Copper jumped down from the bed, his collar jangling. He did not want to call his mother. She'd wish him Merry Christmas, and he'd have to say it back to her. He was honestly shocked she hadn't sent him pictures of her tree, but she had gotten a new phone recently, so she probably didn't know how.

Pepper jumped down too, and Theo stood up. "Come on, Scout," he said to the third dog. "Time to go out." He didn't bother with the boots or his coat. He simply went down the hall and around the corner and let the dogs out. Scout came along last, barely moving. "You can't be an old man already," Theo teased him, and Scout threw him a baleful look as if he understood English.

Theo wished he could nudge the little dog along with his foot, because it was mighty cold outside. A sort of blue grayness hugged the sky as dawn didn't seem to be far off. Theo took care of his own business while the dogs were outside, and when he went to let them back in, all three of them waited at the door.

"Good boys," he said to them as they came rushing in with wet paws and snouts. He gave them a cursory drying-off and went to lay down on the couch. For some reason, he didn't want to go upstairs yet. He didn't need to caffeinate himself first thing in the morning, and maybe he could doze with the TV on.

Two of the puppies jumped up and laid on his side, but Copper lay down on the floor in front of Theo. He didn't care. He was just glad they'd stuck close by. Sometimes Pepper would go upstairs and sniff around, trying to find trouble. Sometimes he found it too, which only encouraged him to try to slink upstairs unattended.

Today, Theo would probably let him. That was how much he didn't want to go upstairs. He wasn't sure why, because Sorrell wasn't even awake yet. He couldn't smell coffee, and he heard no footsteps. He wanted to see her, so she wasn't the reason.

"Maybe it'll be nice to spend the day alone," he whispered to himself. He dislodged the dogs so he could go get his quilt, because it was far too cold in the basement of the cabin to try to go back to sleep without it.

He covered up and got all three dogs on his hip and side, and closed his eyes. Relief cascaded through him. His eyes hurt; that was how tired he was. Theo had dealt with physical exhaustion in the past. This was something different.

With his puppy pals nearby, his body warm and comfortable, and the television on, Theo drifted right back to sleep.

The next time he knew something was happening was when one of the dogs barked. A shrill, startling sound that had Theo flinching and gearing up to curse at whichever canine had dared vocalize his opinion.

"It's just me, you silly thing," Sorrell said.

Theo groaned as he opened his eyes, because there was plenty of light streaming into them now. Not purely natural light, though there were two windows on the wall behind the couch.

"Sorry," Sorrell said, her voice getting closer. "I just came to make sure you guys were all right. It's almost noon."

Theo's heart palpitated. "It is?" He tried opening his eyes again, this time with a bit more success. Sorrell's pretty face still swam in front of him. A lightning bolt of heat shot through him when her fingers brushed his hair off his forehead, leaving a trail of fire in the wake of her touch.

"You must be hungry," she said. "Did you want me to make a lunch-type thing like I did yesterday?"

"If you want," Theo said, pulling his arms out of his blanket and reaching for her. Even with blurry vision and half-closed eyes, his hands knew where to go, and he drew Sorrell to him for a kiss. He didn't let it last too long, because he hadn't exactly brushed his teeth yet that morning.

"Your hair is really long," she said next. "I could cut it for you today, if you'd like."

That got him to focus, and Theo finally met her gaze. "You could?"

"Sure," she said with that smile he adored stuck to her lips. "If you want."

Theo wanted a lot of things, and a haircut by Sorrell sure would be nice. "All right," he said. "Give me a few minutes to get up, and I'll come upstairs."

Sorrell got to her feet and picked up one of the puppies. "I'm taking Scout," she said. "I'm lonely upstairs by myself." She laughed lightly and left, her footsteps soft on the carpeted stairs. Theo watched her go, his heart filling with appreciation for her.

There'd been no *Merry Christmas, Theo*. No mention of a special holiday meal, though he'd had honey-glazed ham at the farmhouse with the Adams' in the past. He dislodged the other two dogs, who both gave him slightly disgruntled looks as they hopped down to the floor and stretched out their hind legs.

He yawned too and decided he could shower now—and get rid of his morning breath—and then go upstairs. With all of that done, he finally made an appearance on the main level of the cabin.

Sorrell had lit a couple of candles and put them on the mantle, and the whole place smelled like frosted sugar cookies—and something that smelled dangerously close to gingerbread. He frowned at the flickering flames from across the room, but turned back to Sorrell when she said, "I opted for something easy today."

Theo took in the nearly spotless kitchen. Dark liquid sat in the coffee pot, but it looked old, like a mixture between sludge and oil. He stepped around her, asking, "Yeah? That's probably good. You don't need to go all-out all the time."

"I'm glad you think so," she said. "Because I literally put a pan of frozen enchiladas in the oven ten minutes ago. They'll be ready in an hour."

"Sounds great," he said. "I love those frozen enchiladas."

"Meanwhile, we can cut your hair, and I know you don't want to do this, but you promised you'd play that new game with me."

Theo groaned as he rinsed out the cold coffee pot and started to make fresh brew.

"Come on," Sorrell needled, her voice light and playful. "I did that video game thing with you."

He chuckled, because she'd been really bad at the trivia game too.

"It's cards," she said. "I know you used to play cards with the cowboys at Chestnut."

"Only once or twice," he said. "And this ain't poker, sweetheart."

"It's better than poker," she said, dancing away from him and around the corner to the pantry.

Theo did not think any card game would be better than poker, and especially not the one Sorrell had bought at the grocery store that had cartoon pictures of sushi on the cards. He got the coffee brewing, and his stomach growled as she re-entered the front of the house.

"Here it is," she said, continuing past the kitchen and to the dining room table. "It says it's a fast game. Twenty minutes."

"Okay," Theo said, because he figured he could do anything for twenty minutes. Before he joined her, though, he pulled open the fridge and got out the container of leftover mashed potatoes and gravy. He stuck that in the microwave and went to stand by the table while she unboxed the game.

He barely listened as she chattered about the rules, and when he finally sat down with his sugared cup of coffee, and his hot potatoes, he was ready for anything.

"All right," she said, tossing cards across the table to him. "Remember, you're looking for three of a kind."

"Mm." Theo looked at his cards, and he had two salmon rolls in bright green kelp. The other card was some sort of fish something-or-other. He wasn't really sure, as Theo wasn't a connoisseur of sushi. He took a bite of potatoes and watched as she laid out three cards.

"You can only take one," she said, peering at the rules as

her voice trailed off. "And you have to put one down too. Any cards you play, you must replace from the draw deck."

Theo was bored already. This felt like a child's game, not something adults would play. He did what she wanted though, and thankfully, she went out only six minutes later.

He beamed at her clear excitement, though he didn't understand it.

"Okay," she said. "Haircut."

He waited on the chair while she went down the hall to the bathroom. She returned empty-handed, and said, "We don't actually have anything to cut your hair with."

Theo twisted and looked up at her. "False promises," he teased. "I see how you are."

Sorrell grinned at him too, and Theo tugged on her hand to get her to sit on his lap. He sighed as she did, wrapping her arms around him and holding his face close to her pulse.

"Sorrell?" he asked.

"Yes, Theo?"

"You want a family, right?"

She leaned away from him, her eyes wide and searching now. "Yes," she said slowly. "Do you?"

"Yes," he said. He simply looked at her, trying to find a reason not to give her the ring he'd bought for her.

It's Christmas, his mind screamed. *And it's not a Christmas gift.*

That was a very good reason.

She won't have anything for you, he thought next, and that was also true. The last thing he wanted to do was make Sorrell feel bad.

"What are you thinking in that head of yours?" she asked, reaching up and pushing her fingers through his hair.

"Nothing," he said.

She didn't like that, if the frown on her face was any indication. Theo didn't know what else to say. He wanted to give her the ring, but he felt like he needed an adequate explanation for why he was doing it on this day, when he'd specifically asked her to skip Christmas with him.

"I'm going to go shower," he said, his thoughts moving in ways he hadn't anticipated. He saw himself down on his knees, showing her the ring, and asking her to marry him.

Sorrell got up, but she didn't move far. "Didn't you already shower?"

"Oh, uh, yeah," he said. "I'll be right back." He went downstairs as quickly as he could, all the dogs following him. Once in the safety of his bedroom, with the door closed and locked and the three puppies on the bed, he paced back and forth.

"What am I doing?" he muttered to himself. "You can't propose to her, Theodore. She's not ready for that, and honestly, neither are you."

Back and forth he went, his mind churning. He couldn't find a single reason why he wasn't ready to propose to Sorrell, and that only scared him further. Thankfully, amidst the chaos of his mind, he remembered his mother had called, and Theo lunged for his phone.

He needed to talk to her right now and find out what he should do about the ring, Sorrell, and his insane desire to make her his fiancée for Christmas.

CHAPTER 16

Sorrell did not like the way Theo conveniently disappeared every time she tried to ask him what he was thinking. He'd done it on the-day-they-could-not-celebrate. He'd scampered downstairs to the basement, and she'd had to call him on the phone to get him to come up and eat the frozen meal she'd put in the oven.

She'd opened a bagged salad and called it Christmas dinner.

Her grandmother would be mortified.

Sorrell was mortified.

But she'd made it through the day.

The day after Christmas, Theo had taken the dogs snow-shoeing. This time, Sorrell stayed at the cabin. She stayed in bed, in fact, because two could play the game of staying on their own level all dang day.

She didn't accomplish anything by doing that though, other than to feel petty and spiteful. She really didn't want to live with those feelings, so she'd swallowed her pride and gone downstairs on the twenty-seventh.

He didn't like her card game, and she could admit it was fairly lame. She didn't like his electronic trivia either. Or snowshoeing. Or the way he asked really personal questions and then cut-and-run when she wanted to know more about what he thought about what she'd asked.

He'd asked about a family, but there had been no follow-up. He'd asked her again about her job. She didn't know. When she asked about Chestnut Ranch, he said two words and went outside with the dogs.

Frustration built beneath her skin, and if Sorrell didn't release it soon, she felt like she might combust. With three days to go until the New Year, Sorrell bundled up in her boots, parka, hat, and gloves, and left the cabin.

Theo had already left to go to town for groceries, and Sorrell had the dogs with her. "Come on," she said to the three of them. "You have to stay by me. I know I'm not as good as Theo." Her mood soured even further. "You have to listen to me anyway."

Scout did, because Scout was practically perfect in every way. He was the most obedient, and he stayed right by her side while Copper and Pepper started running along the paths in the snow they'd made previously. They'd come back to her side, Sorrell knew. They did for Theo, at least, and while she couldn't whistle the way he could, he'd trained them well. She lived with them too, and she fed them bits of chicken from her plate, the same as Theo did.

Sorrell wasn't one for walking up and down hills, especially when the air threatened to freeze her lungs together with every breath. She simply needed some wide open space today. She wasn't even sure why—Theo wasn't in the house. She also didn't mind it when Theo was in the house.

"Yes, you do," she muttered to herself as she kept one eye on Copper. She did, because Theo had stopped talking a few days ago. He'd say the tip of what was on his mind and that was all. She wanted him to say more. At the ranch, he had. She'd always felt like he had anyway. They'd shared real things with each other. Here, Sorrell felt like Theo was holding back.

"Maybe that's just because you have a real relationship now," she said to the empty air around her. "Before, you were just friends. You kept him in a box, and he followed your rules."

There were no rules now, and Sorrell simply didn't know how to operate out here in the wide openness of a romantic relationship with Theo. She knew she felt frustrated and like she was failing every step of the way.

She felt like Theo had boxed himself up and was unwilling to open the flaps.

She went to the end of the street, whistled, and turned around to go back to the cabin. The sun shone overhead, and Sorrell did enjoy the bright rays of it. Mother Nature had spent plenty of time dropping snow over the past few weeks, but she'd taken a break since Christmas Eve. None of it had melted, though, and Sorrell had heard chatter around town that the snow didn't melt until May.

May.

Sorrell usually wore cutoffs and tank tops in Texas in May. She had no idea how to live the winter life, and she didn't want to learn how. The cabin was a nice retreat, and somewhere Sorrell would like to visit again—just not in the winter.

She could imagine this mountain in the summer, and it was green and glorious, with a pure blue sky overhead and plenty of brown in the form of tree trunks and dirt and the wood on the exterior of every home she'd seen up here.

The houses down the canyon were of the normal variety, but the town of Beaver Creek had just as much snow as this cabin community.

Sorrell's nose ran by the time she returned to the cabin, and as it thawed in the warmth of the kitchen, she realized how frozen it had been. She hung up all of her clothes and washed her hands. Her phone rang while she was nice and sudsy, and she dove for it.

She knew then how desperate she was to have someone to talk to, and she hoped it would be Sarena. She liked to talk, and she could keep Sorrell going for quite a long time. Serendipity let Sorrell talk and talk too, and she should be used to talking to someone who didn't do a lot of talking back.

Somehow, when it was Theo, though, the fact that he didn't tell her what was really on his mind annoyed her and frustrated her.

Theo's name sat on the screen, and Sorrell found herself frowning at her device. She didn't feel like risking getting her phone wet and soapy to talk to Theo, so she went back to the sink to finish washing her hands.

It stopped ringing, and Sorrell looked out the window, regret lancing through her. She reached for the kitchen towel hanging from the oven handle when her phone rang again.

Theo—again.

She swiped it on with her still-damp knuckle and tapped the speaker icon. "Hey," she said. "Sorry, I was washing my hands, and I couldn't get the phone."

"It's okay," he said, his voice bright and full of cheer. "I was just wondering if you wanted to have a New Year's Eve party."

Sorrell's mind blanked at the word *party*. "Yes," she blurted out, the first word that came into her mouth. "Yes, a party sounds fun."

Theo chuckled. "I suppose we've been a little somber the past few days," he said. "I'm thinking of getting a piñata..."

"They have a piñata at the grocery store?"

"Yeah," he said, laughing. "I know it's just the two of us, and I promise I won't fight you for the candy."

Sorrell giggled too, and that introduced the first ray of real joy back into her life. People went through ups and downs in their lives—in their day. It was okay for Theo to withdraw sometimes.

"Sounds fun," Sorrell said. "Get a lot of M&M's too. All the different kinds you can, and we can open a new variety every hour until we hit midnight."

"I don't remember the last time I saw midnight," Theo said with a laugh.

"Yeah, you're passed out on the couch by nine-thirty," she teased.

"Hey, those dogs go out *early*."

"Sure," Sorrell said, glancing down at the trio of dogs waiting near the edge of the kitchen. "I took them for a walk today."

"You did not," Theo drawled, his voice deep and throaty.

"I did," Sorrell said. "All the way to the end of the road and back."

"I'm impressed," Theo said.

Sorrell laughed then, because what he'd just said was ridiculous. "If me walking to the end of the road impresses you, I must be the most pathetic person on the planet."

"I didn't mean that," Theo said.

Sorrell didn't say anything else, because she didn't know what to say. She wasn't sure she could say it past the pinch in her throat anyway. She hadn't cried for weeks, but the dam was about to break.

"Lots of M&Ms," Theo said, his voice strained now. "Lots of different varieties."

"Yes," she said, glad her voice had been able to get that single word out without any emotion.

"Anything else?"

Sorrell bent down and picked up Scout, using the dog's calm energy to soothe herself as she moved into the living room and sat on the couch. She sighed and said, "We always had a lot of dips on New Year's Eve. Do you like chips and dip? Crackers and dip?"

"Sure," Theo said.

"Then get a lot of cream cheese, sour cream, and cheese. You know what?" Sorrell asked. "I'll send you a list right now."

"Okay," he said.

"Okay." Sorrell waited a few seconds, and when he didn't say anything else, she said, "See you soon."

"Yeah," he said, and she ended the call.

She quickly tapped out what she needed to make the hot chicken dip she loved, as well as a ranch and bacon cheeseball, and a green onion artichoke dip that she hadn't tasted in far too long.

Theo sent back a picture of his cart, where he had no less than a dozen sharing size packages of M&Ms with the caption, *I got every kind they had.*

Sorrell smiled at the same time a sob worked its way out of her mouth. She wasn't even sure why she was crying, only that she needed to, and she knew once she finished she'd feel so much better.

* * *

Sometime later, she rolled toward her closed bedroom door as all three dogs started barking. "Theo's back, isn't he?" she asked them.

Pepper came sprinting over to her, barking as if someone dangerous was about to blow through the house and steal her away.

"I know," she said. "Theo's back. Now shush."

Scout tried to jump up on the bed, but he didn't quite

make it, and he flopped back to the ground with a whimper.

"Oh, you poor thing," Sorrell said, reaching over the edge of the bed where she was laying. "Come lay by me."

Scout curled right into her chest while Pepper continued to yip at the door. Copper had settled down, but a whine came out of his mouth every few seconds. Sorrell's heart pounded in her chest, because she should go see if Theo needed help carrying in the groceries he'd gone to get.

They sometimes went down to town together and did their shopping. Today, though, he'd texted her early to say he was going without the dogs and would she mind caring for them. He'd been gone for hours and hours—way longer than it took to get groceries—and Sorrell wanted to know what he'd been doing.

He'd called while she'd been shopping and asked her for her ring size, but she'd seen no ring yet. She hated that she'd been expecting to see one. If Theo knew what a simple question like that would do to a woman, he was cruel for asking.

Sorrell reasoned that he didn't know that his quick phone call that day had kept her awake every night since. She'd let her mind imagine a fairytale where Theo knelt in front of her and asked her to marry him. She'd scratched that scenario out of her mind as quickly as she could, because he'd not brought up the subject of marriage—yet.

"Sorrell?" he called, his voice coming through the closed door easily. Pepper barked again, and Copper whined. Seeing no other choice, Sorrell got up, a sigh pulling through her whole chest.

"You guys are so annoying," she said to the dogs. "I took

good care of you today, and all you can do is whine to go see *him*." She opened the door, and Pepper and Copper practically tripped over one another to be the first one out onto the loft. Even Scout jumped down from the bed and followed them at a trot, his tail held high as he went.

"Traitor," Sorrell said under her breath. She took a deep breath and left the room too, tucking her hands into the front pocket of her hoodie. She leaned over the railing of the loft, where she could see the whole living room, dining area, and part of the peninsula in the kitchen. The countertop she could see held many bags, and a thread of guilt stitched through her.

"I'll be down in a second," she called.

Theo was laughing as he bent over with all the dogs trying to get him to pat them first. "Okay," he said, not looking up at her.

Sorrell went back into her bedroom and closed the door. She leaned her back against it, trying to decide what to do.

She'd stopped crying a while ago, and she'd washed her face since. She wasn't worried about Theo knowing about her break down. She was allowed to cry. She'd cried in front of him plenty of times.

The difference was that she had never cried in front of him *because* of him. She'd always been able to explain herself to him, and he'd always been a safe place to fall for her. She hadn't anticipated him being the *reason* she needed a safe place, and she honestly didn't know what to do next.

"Sorrell?" His voice sounded so close, and a couple of knocks scared her away from the door where she'd been

standing. "Come see the piñata, sugar." He sounded so glee-
ful, and Sorrell smoothed down her hair and took a deep
breath.

She opened the door, a smile hitched in place. "You and
this—oh."

He held up a brightly colored object. Sorrell had no idea
what it was, but the crepe paper on it came in red, orange,
yellow, and tan. "What is that?"

"It's a rat," he said, his smile stretching across his whole
face. "They had all this Chinese New Year stuff. It's the year
of the rat this year."

"Oh," Sorrell said again. "That's so...great."

Theo laughed as he lowered his arm, the giant party rat
going with it. "Come on down, sugar. I need your help with
everything." His eyes met hers, and Sorrell couldn't tell
him no.

She stepped out of her bedroom and past him, going
down the steps first. He followed, telling her about the other
things he'd got to "liven up the cabin."

Sorrell took a few steps toward the kitchen and stopped,
taking in the bags and bags and bags of things he'd carried in.
The entire kitchen counter was covered, as was the dining
table that could seat six.

"What all did you get?" she asked, glancing around at the
sheer enormity of what he'd purchased that morning.

"So much," he said as he stopped beside her. "But first, I
wanted to give you this."

After a few seconds where Sorrell tried to process what
she was seeing, she turned toward him.

He held a black velvet ring box in his hand and wore the happy-go-lucky smile on his face that she'd seen multiple times before.

She stared at him for an extra moment, and then let her eyes drop to the ring box. She couldn't make herself move to take it from him.

CHAPTER 17

Theo's pulse beat with the sound of a gong in his ears, the rhythm of which increased the longer Sorrell stood there. "It's not a snake," he said, making his voice light.

"What is it?" she asked.

"It's a ring." He opened the box and glanced at the ring. It was still as beautiful as all the other times he'd opened the box and taken it in. He turned it toward her so she could see it. "I got it at this specialty shop. I know you don't wear a ton of jewelry, but I thought you'd like this. It's buffalo turquoise, and there's only one mine in the whole world."

Sorrell hadn't looked up from the ring box, so Theo kept going. "I got this one, because it seemed like your style. It's black and white, which will go with whatever you're wearing to the community center each day."

He commanded himself to stop talking, because it was pretty presumptuous of him to think she'd want to wear his ring every day. *It's not your ring*, he corrected himself mentally.

"Say something," he said as the silence went on and on.

Sorrell finally looked up, her eyes wide and full of either fear or anxiety. Theo thought he detected some hope in there too. "It's beautiful," she said.

"You really think so?"

"Yes," she said, a genuine smile touching her face. She'd been faking with him upstairs, and Theo wondered what had really happened that morning at the cabin. She'd sounded happy enough on the phone earlier, but his last few texts to her had gone unread.

He took the ring out of the box and asked, "Which finger do you want it on?"

She held out her right hand, and he slid it on her fourth finger. It fit like a glove, and Sorrell held her hand out, a look of adoration on her face. "It's wonderful." She looked up at him again, this time stepping into his personal space and wrapping her arms around him. "Thank you."

He drew her tightly against his chest, all of the things that had rattled loose in the past few days finally settling back where they belonged. "I thought of you when I saw it," he said. "It made buying it really easy."

Her hands slid over his shoulders to his face, and she pulled his face close to hers. "We're okay, right, Theo?"

Her whisper nearly undid all of his willpower, but his question concerned her too. "Of course we are, sweetheart. Why wouldn't we be?"

She closed her eyes, but Theo wanted an answer, so he

didn't lean in for the kiss he so desperately wanted. "Sorrell?" he asked.

"I feel like you disappeared the last few days," she said. "I asked you things, and you disappeared downstairs."

Everything froze inside Theo, except his thoughts. They raced, and he tried to find the one that would reassure her that he hadn't run away from *her*.

"I want you to tell me what's inside your head," she said, swaying in his arms. He liked the feel of her hands on the sides of his face and neck. They were cold, and he was hot, and he seized onto the temperature difference between them.

"It's not pretty in there," he said. "I just needed a couple of days to disappear, I suppose."

"What are you thinking right now?"

"I'm thinking that I'm thrilled you loved the ring, and I want to kiss you for a while before we unpack all the groceries." He smiled, glad when a small smile adorned her face too. She opened her eyes and looked at him, her thumb running along his bottom lip.

"What are you thinking, sugar?" he asked.

"I'm thinking I can't wait to bust open that piñata on New Year's Eve, and I'm thinking that I honestly can't wait until we get back to Chestnut Springs."

An alarm went off in Theo's head. "Why's that?"

"Don't you think this feels a little too...fake?" she asked. "It's like a dream, and we can't live inside a dream forever, Theo."

He wanted to tease her and ask her if she was sure. Instead, he erased the distance she'd put between them. "It's not fake for me," he said, peering down at her. "Is it fake for you, Sorrell?"

"Oh, don't start calling me Sorrell," she said, tipping her head back. "Kiss me, cowboy, and then let's get the groceries unpacked."

Theo did what she said, his heart warming at the *cowboy* endearment. She'd never called him that before, and he sure did like it.

"Is that straight?" she asked hours later as she balanced on her tip-toes on one of the dining room chairs. He'd bought a banner that read *Happy New Year* in black and silver letters, and they were draping it across the front windows of the cabin.

He stood back and evaluated both sides of the banner. "Looks good," he said, and Sorrell pressed the tape all the way to the wall. They'd spent several minutes kissing, and then Theo had spent the next few minutes reassuring her that the space he needed was not space from her. They'd put away all of the groceries he'd bought, and he'd shown her all of the decorations he'd bought.

She laughed at him and said there was no way they'd be able to use it all. Theo had set out to prove her wrong, and he'd managed to find a spot for every banner, sign, and bauble that he'd bought.

The colorful rat now dangled from the bottom of the loft, and Sorrell kept eyeing it like it would come to life and attack her in the night. She'd called it "creepy," but Theo loved it. The moment he'd laid eyes on it at the grocery store, the entire New Year's Eve party had come to life inside his head. Minus the menu, because Sorrell would be in charge of that.

In so many ways, Sorrell was in charge of Theo's whole life, and he disliked that he'd put distance between them. He suspected she'd been crying that day, because no matter how much she covered her face and eyes in powders and creams, Theo could tell when she wasn't happy.

She'd perked up since their talk, but Theo had kept one eye on her as the decorating began. She sighed as she got down from the chair. "That's it," she said. She came to stand beside him, and he draped his arm around her shoulders as they surveyed the cabin together.

Black, silver, and gold dripped from every available surface, and their party favors and top hats waited on the table for the big night. She'd detailed the menu—plenty of finger foods, crackers and dips, and chips and dips. All things Theo absolutely loved, and with Sorrell cooking, everything would be delicious.

"What are we going to do for our last week here?" she asked.

"I don't know," Theo said. "Maybe you can make some of those homemade marshmallows you're always bragging about, and we'll have a different flavor of hot chocolate every day."

"I do *not* brag about them," Sorrell said with a giggle. She nudged him with her hip, and they laughed together. "I think you're going to need every spare minute to get all these decorations down before we have to leave this place."

"Probably," Theo said, but he didn't care. He loved the decorations, and he loved that he didn't have to deal with Christmas again for three hundred and sixty-two more days.

Three days later, Sorrell came downstairs from the third floor about eight, the same time she did most mornings. Theo glanced up from his phone. "It's New Year's Eve," he said, standing up.

"You're kidding." Sorrell threw him a smile on her way into the kitchen. Theo wanted to kiss her good morning and good night. He'd definitely need a nap if he was going to make it all the way to midnight.

He wrapped his arms around Sorrell from behind and took a deep breath of the scent of her hair. She always smelled faintly like flowers, and today, he got a whiff of the lavender fresh dryer sheets she loved so much.

He swept her hair off her shoulder and place a kiss against her neck, everything male inside him firing on all cylinders now.

"Mm," she said, pressing into his touch.

"I want my New Year's Eve kiss now," he whispered.

Sorrell turned easily in his arms and tipped her head back to receive his kiss. Theo forced himself to go slow and stay present in the moment. He pulled away far sooner than he would've liked and gathered her close to his chest. "It's going to be a great year," he said. "I can feel it."

"Is that right?" she asked. "What do you feel when you feel that?"

"I don't know," he said. "Like, this magic in the air."

She giggled against his chest, but she made no move to try to escape the circle of his arms. She quieted quickly, and Theo did too. He wondered what this year would actually bring for the two of them.

He'd spoken to his mother about Sorrell a few days ago, and he'd confessed that he might be in love with her. His mom had told him to get down on his knees and ask the Lord what he should do. Theo wasn't nearly as religious as his mother, but he'd done what she'd suggested.

He'd never heard a voice from On High or witnessed a chorus of angels. Deep down in his soul, though, he felt that he and Sorrell should be together.

Was that love?

He wasn't sure.

Theo had never truly been in love with a woman before, and he wasn't exactly sure what that looked like and felt like. With Sorrell, he was comfortable, but did that mean he loved her?

He could easily look at Pepper or Scout and know he loved those silly dogs. Copper too. They loved him right back; he could feel it from them. They listened to him. They laid by him all day. They followed him everywhere he went —even into the bathroom.

He took care of them. They provided something for him.

He didn't want to compare himself and Sorrell to the puppies, but he also wanted to take care of her. She took care of him by feeding him and letting him nap in the afternoons and supporting him in whatever decisions he made in his life.

"Sorrell?" he asked.

"Yeah?"

"Have you ever been in love before?"

She sucked in a breath and backed out of his arms. Her eyes were as round as dinner plates, and Theo fell back a couple of steps until his back hit the peninsula. "I'm not saying anything," he said. "I'm just wondering."

She nodded, her head almost bobbling on her neck. "Yes," rasped out of her throat. "I was in love with this guy named Cameron Carlisle once." She folded her arms, but she didn't look away from him. "Utterly in love with him. He was a cowboy too, and he's the reason I—" Her voice seemed to mute in the middle of a word, and Theo simply waited while she swallowed.

Her throat worked and worked, and finally she managed to say, "He's the reason I told you no so many times." She looked away then, quickly reaching up with one hand to swipe at her eyes.

Theo made no move to comfort her. "He broke your heart," he said. He hadn't known it in the beginning, but as time went on, and he got to know Sorrell better, he could sense something traumatic had happened in her past.

"Into a million pieces," she said. "I thought he loved me too, but he had this new opportunity in the rodeo circuit." She sniffed and wiped her eyes again. "And the next thing I knew, he'd packed and left Chestnut Springs." She snapped her fingers, and though the sound wasn't loud, it almost filled the kitchen like a gunshot. "He was gone, and I was left wondering if he'd ever come back."

"I'm assuming he didn't."

Sorrell shook her head, her attention away somewhere out the window. "He didn't, even when I called and begged him to." She inhaled slowly, and Theo was impressed her eyes had dried out already. "I even offered to come be with him where he was. He said—" She coughed and cleared her throat. "He said he didn't want me." Sorrell lowered her head and scuffed at something on the floor with her toes.

Theo wanted her, and he had for a long time.

"I want you, Sorrell," he said, his voice very low and very serious.

Slowly, her eyes lifted to meet his. "You do?"

"Yes."

She hurried into his arms and kissed him with tears running down her cheeks. "I've wanted to tell you about him," she said. "He's held me back for so long, and I hate that I let him come between us for so many years."

"It's okay," Theo whispered, hoping to reassure her. "It's fine, Sorrell. Nothing's been lost."

"I'm so sorry," she said again and then again. She finally quieted, and Theo simply held her close.

"It's going to be a great year," he said again. "Starting

today. Okay, sugar? We're going to *make* it a great year." His determination and will to do just that solidified in that moment. He would do whatever it took to keep Sorrell in his life this year, and he couldn't help wondering if the two of them would be husband and wife by this time next year.

The thought warmed him as much as it made him want to retreat to the lower level of the cabin to give himself space to think.

Sorrell didn't like it when he disappeared, so he stayed in the kitchen with her, a silent prayer in his heart that he could do the right thing when it came to Sorrell and her fragile heart.

CHAPTER 18

Sorrell went up the steps again, hoping this would be the last time. She and Theo had been taking their stuff from the cabin for at least an hour. She'd been packing for three days. Every time she thought she had everything, she'd remember that she'd once used the main level bathroom and left her bathrobe in there. Or that she'd come in from outside through the basement level, and she'd left her boots and hat down there.

They hadn't been speaking much, and Sorrell sighed as she entered the cabin again.

"Got it all?" Theo asked. He'd had his truck packed for maybe five minutes, and he stood in the kitchen with a cup of coffee in his hands.

"Yeah," she said. "I think so." She sat at the peninsula and looked at him. "It's a long drive."

"Only seven hours today," he said with a smile. He loved road trips, and he said the only thing that would make this one better was if she could somehow ride with him. But she'd driven her car from Chestnut Springs, and she had to drive it back. "I'll take you to dinner in Amarillo. There's a great Tex-Mex place there. I stopped on the way through."

Sorrell smiled at him and nodded. "All right."

"I'm going to call about a trailer too," he said. "Then we can ride together tomorrow."

"You don't have to do that," she said. "I can drive." She'd made it to the cabin in the top of the Rocky Mountains, hadn't she?

"I'm going to call anyway," he said. "My truck might not be big enough though."

"Are you kidding? That thing is a monster."

Theo chuckled as he shook his head. He sipped his coffee, and Sorrell got to her feet. "I'm going to use the bathroom one more time and make sure we've done everything on the check-out list. Then we should go."

They'd agreed to be on the road by nine, so they could grab lunch after a few hours and then be in Amarillo before dark. Sorrell could drive at night too, believe it or not, but Theo didn't want a late start. He was supposed to meet with Seth Johnson tomorrow night, almost the moment he returned to Chestnut Springs, and Sorrell didn't envy him for that.

She just wanted to be in her own house and sleep in her own bed. *Only one more night*, she thought. After she'd used the restroom and washed her hands, she picked up the binder in the kitchen. "Let's see...strip the beds and put the sheets by the laundry room."

"Did that," Theo said.

"Empty the fridge." They'd done that. "Lights off. You turned off the water main behind the water heater?"

"Yes, ma'am."

"Dishes in the dishwasher, and we need to start it before we go."

"Yep." Theo opened the machine and put his mug inside. He bent to get a dishwashing pod out from under the sink and accomplished that too.

"Nest at sixty-nine degrees." She stepped over to the Wi-Fi thermostat and noted that it was right at sixty-nine. "I think we've got it."

"Garbage out," he said. "I checked the pantry too. We're good."

Sorrell put the binder on the counter and looked at him again. "I'm excited to go home, but I don't want to leave at the same time."

Theo took her easily into his arms. "I know exactly how you feel." He wrapped her up tight, and Sorrell let her eyes drift closed as she snuggled into the warmth and strength of his chest. They swayed together, and it was moments like this that Sorrell didn't want to end.

When she returned to Chestnut Springs, she'd have one full day before she was expected back at the community center. Dread filled her, and she was suddenly looking forward to the thirteen-hour drive in front of her.

"Let's do this," she said. "I'll follow you."

Theo stepped away from her, his smile stuck to his face. "Right. The moment we hit the freeway, you'll be off like a shot. I know how fast you drive." He laughed, and Sorrell didn't deny it. She couldn't help the restlessness she felt in the car. Sometimes she wished she lived in a time where she could transport from place to place. If that existed now, she'd have been able to step out of the cabin and enjoy Christmas with her sisters on the ranch for a couple of hours, and Theo wouldn't have even known.

She let him lead them down the canyon, and he pulled in to get gas. She did too, and he wrapped her in his arms and kissed her right there by the pumps. "See you in Amarillo, okay?" he asked, his voice soft and tender. "I'll probably stop a couple of times for the dogs."

"Okay," she said.

"You know where the hotel is?"

"Yes, sir." She beamed up at him. "I'll see you there." Her car filled faster than his, and she left him at the gas station and faced the open road in front of her. She wasted no time before calling her sister, and Sarena picked up with a laugh.

"Are you on the way home?" she asked after a moment.

"Yes," Sorrell said. "What's so funny?"

"One of the new ranch hands can do these amazing impressions," she said as a round of laughter sounded behind her.

Sorrell couldn't help smiling too. "Paul, right?"

"Yeah," Sarena said, still giggling. "I can't wait until you get back."

"Sure," Sorrell said. "What have you missed about me?" Now that Sarena had her separate life, with a baby and a husband, Sorrell didn't see her as much as she once had.

"Your pretty face," Sarena said, plenty of happiness in her voice.

Sorrell burst out laughing, because she knew exactly what Sarena had missed. "It's the leftovers, isn't it?" she asked as she quieted.

"I hadn't even *thought* of those," Sarena teased.

"I'm not cooking for at least a week once I get back," Sorrell said. "I'm exhausted."

"I thought you went to the cabin to relax and unwind," Sarena said.

"I did that, too."

"But you're tired?"

"Yeah."

"Why?"

"Is it...this much work to be married to Darren?" Sorrell asked, sudden worry threading through her. "I'm constantly thinking about what I said, and if I should've said it. I'm worried I did something wrong, or if he's just quiet because he's tired too." Sorrell exhaled heavily, the winter landscape in front of her beautiful but boring. "I don't know. I think too much about stuff."

"But did you cry about it?" Sarena asked.

"Only a couple of times," Sorrell said, her pride filling her. "I did really good, Sarena."

"I'm glad," her sister said. "Try not to think too hard, Sorrell. I'm a little surprised you didn't call to say you and Theo were engaged."

"What?" Sorrell demanded. "You're kidding, right?"

"Why would I be kidding?" Sarena really didn't sound like she was joking either.

Sorrell blinked rapidly, her thoughts flying around in such a way that she couldn't grab onto any of them. "Is that what Serendipity thought?"

"I don't—"

"Don't lie to me," Sorrell said, her voice hard.

"Yes," Sarena said, her voice hushing. "We've talked about it, and we thought you'd be engaged. You're not engaged, I take it?"

"No," Sorrell practically barked. "I mean, he bought me a ring, but it's not a wedding ring." She glanced down at the black and white stone on her right ring finger. She loved the ring with her whole soul, and not just because Theo had purchased it for her. It represented so much more than that. It showed her how well he knew her, and Sorrell took her hands off the wheel for a moment to move the ring from her right hand to her left.

The opaque stone wasn't anywhere near a diamond, but Sorrell certainly could get used to wearing a ring on this finger. At the same time, her heart pounded loudly in her chest. It almost hurt, it beat so hard.

"Yes, you sent us a picture of the ring," Sarena said. "It's beautiful."

The conversation stalled, and Sorrell wanted to talk to herself. "I better go," she said. "I'll see you tomorrow night."

"We're getting pizza," Sarena said. "We'll have everyone here, so you don't have to clean up afterward."

"Thank you, Sarena," Sorrell said, and she tapped on the icon on her phone to disconnect the call. "Engaged," she immediately scoffed.

Horror wound through her as she considered how many other people had probably thought the same thing. Sorrell had run off with her boyfriend for six weeks, and when she got back, she'd be engaged.

How humiliating.

"And worse," she said to herself. "Showing up *not* engaged. Then they'll all wonder what's wrong with you. Or him."

Her fingers released the steering wheel and then gripped it again. Her skin felt prickly and like she needed to scratch every inch of it. Her mind would not settle, and Sorrell couldn't latch onto something to do to get this nervous buzz out of her system.

Eventually, the noise in her head quieted. The snow gave way to endless plains, the color of khaki stretching forever. She drove through somewhere for lunch in a tiny town, the name of which she didn't catch. She blinked, and she was practically by it.

By the time she pulled into the hotel, the sun's light had started to wane, her legs felt like someone had replaced them with sticks of wood, and she couldn't stand listening to the same pop song for a tenth time.

Theo had made their room reservations, and the woman behind the desk wouldn't let Sorrell give her credit card and go up to one of the rooms. She had to call Theo, and he spoke to the woman, who eyed Sorrell like she'd stolen the tall, broad-shouldered cowboy's identity and was trying to get a free room for one night.

After a twenty-minute ordeal, Sorrell had to work incredibly hard not to let her impatience and annoyance show. Thankfully, she'd had plenty of meetings where she'd sat there and literally counted as high as she could as people more important than her droned on and on.

A sigh of relief filled her as she finally entered the room and let the door swing closed behind her. She showered and dressed in the nicest clothes she'd brought—a pair of dark blue jeans and a navy blue sweater with white stripes.

She'd spent loads of time with Theo, but they had a date tonight, and Sorrell wanted to look nice.

An hour later, Theo knocked on her door, and Sorrell had never been happier that she'd showered, dressed nice, and perfumed herself when she opened the door and saw Theo standing there.

He also wore a pair of dark-wash jeans, a black polo, and a leather jacket over that. With his cowboy hat—which he hadn't worn every day in the cabin—he was easily the handsomest man Sorrell had ever laid eyes on.

Her heart did that rapid, loud beating again, and she pressed one hand to her chest to try to calm it.

"Howdy, sugar," he drawled.

Sorrell giggled, the rest of this day disappearing under Theo's good mood.

"You ready to eat?"

Her stomach grumbled at her, and she said, "Absolutely." She stepped out into the hallway with him, and he reached for her hand. She squeezed his, and he glanced at her out of the corner of his eye. "Good drive?"

"I got here," she said, everything she'd been stewing about for the past eight hours roaring back to life. "Were you aware, Theo, that my sisters—and who knows who else— thought we'd return to Chestnut Springs *engaged*?"

Theo slowed as they approached the elevator. He reached out with his free hand and pushed the button before he looked at her. His eyes were serious and dark, and Sorrell wasn't sure what to make of that. "I wasn't aware of that, no."

Sorrell straightened her shoulders and shook her hair so it all cascaded down her back. "Sarena told me." She shook her head. "Ridiculous."

The elevator arrived with a ding, and Sorrell started to get on it. Theo didn't come with her, and her fingers slipped out of his. She turned back, half on the elevator and half off. "You're not coming?"

He wore a perfect storm on his face, the joy and smile from moments ago completely gone. "You think being engaged to me is ridiculous?"

Sorrell opened her mouth to protest, but nothing came out.

CHAPTER 19

"Of course not," Sorrell said, but Theo had seen the hesitation. He couldn't get himself to move, because everything in his life was crashing down around him.

The past couple of months in Colorado had been some of the best of his life, and she thought their relationship was ridiculous?

Her mouth moved as she kept talking, but Theo couldn't hear her. He'd booked two rooms at the hotel for tonight, and they were right next to each other. He didn't even want to be in the same state as Sorrell right now.

"Theo?" Her voice finally punctured the white noise in his ears. She'd gotten off the elevator, and no one had pushed the button again. "Are you okay?"

"No," he said truthfully. "I don't feel very well." He just wanted to get away from her. Had he been deluding himself all this time?

"We don't have to go," she said. "They have room service here. We'll order and watch a movie in your room."

Theo looked at her, sure he hadn't heard her right. "Sorrell...I don't know what to say." He took a step back, needing some distance to get his thoughts in line. "I actually thought we were serious."

"I just said that," Sorrell said. "Were you listening?"

"I heard you say being engaged to me would be ridiculous, and then I watched you hesitate when I asked you about it."

"I didn't hesitate."

"Yes, you did." He continued to walk backward. "Right there, you didn't. But a few seconds ago, you did. You opened your mouth, and nothing came out, and then you had to reset yourself. I've seen you do that before, Sorrell."

She did it when she needed a minute to smooth over her annoyance and deal with a difficult personality at work. He'd seen her do it when she was irritated with her sister, and he'd seen her do it with him when he'd asked her out once again.

Fool, he thought, the word shouting in his head.

"Theo," she said from behind him, and Theo hadn't even realized he'd turned around and started walking. "Wait."

"It's okay," he said, mostly to himself. If he could just get back to the room, he could figure out what to do. He didn't have to stay here tonight. He could drive through the night. Maybe he should go to Georgia to visit his mother.

"Theo," she said, her voice desperate now. It sounded much farther away, but Theo wouldn't be able to get his door unlocked and get inside without her catching up to him. He pulled his keycard out of his back pocket anyway, a prayer starting somewhere in the back of his mind.

"It's fine, Sorrell," he said. "I just didn't realize you were playing with me."

"I'm not."

"It's okay," he said. "I mean, I get it. Here's foolish Theo, hanging on to your every word and every glance for literally years. I'm such a loser." He felt himself spiraling, but he couldn't stop. All he could do now was hope he made it inside his room before he said something he'd regret later.

"Wait," she said. "None of that is true."

He held his keycard against the pad, anxious for the light to turn green. It did just as she slid in front of him. "Stop, please."

Theo glared down at her, every nerve ending in his body screaming at him. "I can't stand the thought of you and me being ridiculous." His voice came out raw and far too high. He couldn't remember the last time he cried, and he wasn't going to break down in front of Sorrell.

"I didn't mean that."

"What did you mean?"

"I meant that it's ridiculous that everyone is talking about us. They have all these unreasonable expectations of us, and—"

"So now a relationship with me is unreasonable."

"That is *not* what I said," Sorrell said, glaring up at him.

Theo stepped back, because he'd never been able to think very clearly with Sorrell so close. "Do you see us together? In five years? Or ten? With kids, and a big house somewhere in the middle of the Hill Country, with one of those gates near the highway that signifies our driveway?"

He watched that indecision roll across her face, and he hated it. He hated everything about the last five minutes. He hated that he'd been thinking long-term when she hadn't.

"I'm going to be sick," he said. "Please move."

"Theo," she said.

Theo's insides shook, and he could not stand to keep looking at her. "I'm going to say something really cruel in a moment, and I'd rather not." He focused on the ground, barely able to see the tips of her boots. "Please, Sorrell, move so I can go into my room."

She moved, and Theo angled his head away from her as he filled the space where she'd been, pressed the keycard to the sensor, waited for the green light, and escaped from the worst humiliation of his life.

"That's right, Ma," he said an hour later, facing the scene out his window. The whole city spread before him, and while Theo had never spent a lot of time in Amarillo, he had a feeling he'd like to. "I've got a flight out of Amarillo in the morning. They're letting me bring the dogs in a kennel, because I bought an extra seat."

"I'm confused, Theo."

He was too. He exhaled, because it had taken all of his remaining strength just to make this phone call. He'd practiced making his voice bright and chipper, as if he had anything to be happy about right now.

"My time at the cabin is up," he said. "I haven't been home in a while, and I thought it would be a good time to come visit." He hadn't called Seth Johnson. He was supposed to meet with the man tomorrow night to go over a contract and get all the hiring paperwork signed.

Theo simply wasn't sure he could do it. Sorrell would go right back to her regular life, working sixty hours a week at the community center. He'd put in longer hours on someone else's ranch.

For what? he asked himself. For nothing. He still didn't have a purpose in his life, despite his money and time and talent.

Maybe he had no talent.

"I've got a hair appointment tomorrow," his mother said, and Theo sighed as he turned away from the twinkling lights in the city.

Pepper looked up and cocked his head, and Theo went to sit beside his dogs. He sank onto the bed, a great gust of air coming out of his mouth. "Okay," he said as all three dogs got up from where they'd piled together to come lean into him as if he were one of them. He reached out absently to rub them. "I'll cancel the ticket. I'll come for your birthday, maybe."

"Sure," she said. "Let's make a plan."

"Okay," Theo said again.

"What's wrong, dear?" she asked, and he felt like he'd finally gotten her attention.

He reached up and rubbed the back of his neck. He couldn't bring himself to tell his mother about the argument with Sorrell. Deep down, he knew it was more than an argument. It went all the way to the foundation of who they were, what they'd been doing, and their entire future together.

"Theodore," his mom said. "You always tell me the truth."

"I broke up with Sorrell," he finally said.

"What?" his mother cried. "Why would you do that?"

The whole story poured out of him then, and reliving it for a second time was just as terrible as the first. "Ridiculous, Ma. What am I supposed to do with that?" He was the ridiculous one, and he couldn't imagine his mother being able to say anything that would make this better. She often helped him see things in a different light, but Theo had already tried to see things from every angle.

He'd managed to walk away from Sorrell without calling her selfish, so that was something. He had a lot more he could say too, and he'd even considered pounding on the door that separated their rooms and demanding the buffalo turquoise ring back. If he didn't mean anything to her, why would she want to keep it?

"I don't know what to say," his mom said. "I haven't met Sorrell, but she doesn't seem like the type of woman to be so unkind."

"Mom, she's told me no at least two dozen times. I should've seen this coming." She was never going to say yes to him, not when it mattered. She was more worried about what others thought of her—of what her sisters might think.

An unending river of pain flowed through him, and he lay back on the bed. "I have to go, Ma," he whispered. "I'll call you later."

"Theo," she said, and he hesitated. She did too, finally saying, "Don't let this define you, boy. She doesn't deserve you if she's going to be embarrassed to be your fiancée."

Theo simply pressed his eyes closed and nodded. "I love you, Ma."

"Love you too, son."

He hung up, letting his hand flop to the bed, where Scout immediately started licking his arm. Theo simply let him, because he didn't have the strength to do much else. Even his mother hadn't had anything positive to say. No reassurances that he wouldn't be alone forever, or that he hadn't wasted the last seven years of his life by pining after a woman who was cruel enough to lead him on and then rip his heart out right when he thought he was about to get what he'd dreamed of for so long.

He hadn't bought her an engagement ring, but it had been on his list of things to do very soon after they returned to Chestnut Springs. He'd actually been worried about taking the job at Chestnut Ranch, because he knew the men there worked long hours, and he wouldn't have time to see Sorrell.

The future he'd started to imagine for him and her faded right behind his closed eyes, and Theo heaved himself back to a sitting position. "All right, guys," he said, and he heard the exhaustion in his own voice. "I can't stay here. Who's up for another drive?"

He hadn't done much unpacking, so it didn't take long to put the few toiletries he'd used to get ready for what he'd anticipated to be a romantic date with his girlfriend back in his bag. He clipped leashes to all the dogs, stuffed his cowboy hat on his head, and left the room.

Downstairs, he simply walked out, all three puppies right at his side like the good boys they were. He didn't have to check-out. He didn't have to answer to anyone.

He drove away from the hotel, intending to stop at the nearest gas station. With that done, he pointed his truck south and east along the highway that would eventually lead him to Chestnut Springs, nestled in the Texas Hill Country that Theo had fallen in love with the very moment he'd seen the area.

His mind went round and round different scenarios. By the time he'd decided not to take the job at Chestnut Ranch, it was far too late to call Seth Johnson and talk to him about it. Theo hated to let the man down, because that wasn't what Theo did. If he said he'd report for work on the ranch at a certain time, he did.

Not only that, when he reached for his phone in the console, it wasn't there. "Great," he said to himself. He'd gone way too far to go back to the hotel and get his phone, and he decided it didn't matter anyway. He had plenty of money. He'd simply buy another phone when he got a chance.

He drove until he couldn't drive anymore, and then he

pulled into the nearest hotel he could find. This room was considerably less nice than the one in Amarillo, and they definitely didn't have room service.

Theo didn't care. He collapsed onto the bed, let the dogs snuggle into his side, and fell asleep.

"Does that sound fair?" Seth looked up from the contract. "I know it's not as much as The Singer Ranch, but—"

"It's fine," Theo said, his voice almost a monotone. He'd slept until almost noon, only waking when housekeeping came in to clean his room. He'd made a hasty exit then, and shown up at Chestnut Ranch only an hour later.

Seth had taken time from his day to show him the cabin where he'd live and then to go over this paperwork with him. He'd said Theo's dogs were welcome anywhere on the ranch, and Theo had said hello to the few cowboys he'd seen as Seth had taken him on a quick tour of the ranch.

He scrawled his name at the bottom of the paper and put the pen down. "Thanks, Seth."

"Sure thing," he said with a big smile. "I'm thrilled you're going to be with us. Sarena Adams had nothing but good things to say about you."

Theo frowned but said nothing.

"So tomorrow," Seth said. "Take today to get settled in the cabin. Do you have anything besides what's in your truck?" Seth turned toward the front of the cabin, though the blinds were closed and his truck couldn't be seen.

"No," Theo said. He too turned toward the front door. Most of what he had in the back of his truck was winter gear, and he didn't need that here. "I can handle it." He just wanted to be alone. He didn't want to shake hands and smile. He didn't want to detail what the cabin had been like and explain that he really had skipped Christmas.

He wished he could skip the last seven years of his life.

Pure misery streamed through him, and he raised his hand in a half-hearted wave as Seth left the cabin. He wasn't even sure what the man had said to him. He looked down at the dogs, knowing he should go bring in some of his stuff.

He didn't want to. "I'm going to take a nap," he said instead. "You guys can join me if you want." The clicking sound of their claws on the hard floor as he went down the short hall to the bedroom brought him more comfort than he could express. They didn't seem to notice that his heart was no longer in his body, but Theo could feel the hollow part of his chest as it grew and expanded endlessly.

CHAPTER 20

Sorrell was crying when she pulled up to the farmhouse where she'd lived her whole life. There were no other cars there, and for once, she was glad to have the huge house to herself. She'd hated it in the past, because Sorrell didn't like being alone for very long.

"Get used to it," she said as she cut the engine and reached for the door handle. "You're going to be alone forever."

As usual, she'd messed up everything between her and Theo. She didn't even know how things had gone from amazing to a break-up in less than five minutes. She knew he hadn't answered a single one of her phone calls or texts—which made sense when she'd found his phone the next morning.

She knew he hadn't slept in the room next to hers. When she'd gone downstairs and claimed he'd lost his key, she'd gotten another one and been able to get inside his room.

The bed hadn't been slept in, but she had found his phone just lying there, all of her notifications on it. There was no lingering scent of his cologne or skin, and Sorrell had lived with him for long enough to know that Theo left evidence of his existence behind.

That was when the tears had started, and Sorrell hadn't been able to curb the tide since. Anger accompanied her inside the farmhouse, and she screamed as she slammed the front door closed behind her as hard as she could.

There was no one there to hear her. Only the humming of the furnace filled the air, and Sorrell sank to her knees, sobbing in full force again.

"I didn't mean our engagement would be ridiculous," she said, her voice not even remotely her own. She'd explained all of this to herself, the landscape along the highway, and the Lord several times already.

"I didn't mean that," she said. "I meant that my sisters were ridiculous, sitting here on the ranch gossiping about me and Theo." She wiped her face, but there was simply too much liquid for her to clear away. "I did not say or mean to imply that a relationship and life with him would be unreasonable. How can he even think that?"

Sorrell didn't know how else to communicate with him. He'd disappeared a few times at the cabin, but she couldn't expect him to be happy and joyful all the time. He'd mourned the death of his father; she knew the toll of that better than anyone.

She'd kissed him so many times. They'd enjoyed many evenings together, and she simply did not understand how

Theo could even consider for one second that she'd led him on, played him, or thought a relationship with him was ridiculous.

Her mind urged her to try to contact him, but she refused to do it. He didn't have a phone, and she would not interrupt him during his meeting with Seth next door—if he'd even gone to Chestnut Ranch.

Sorrell did manage to pick herself up off the floor, and she went into the kitchen.

This farmhouse was so familiar to her, she could walk around it in complete blackness and know right where she was. Theo had spoken true that she hadn't considered a life outside of this house, or beyond the fences of this ranch.

He hadn't brought it up either. She didn't even know he'd been thinking about proposing or getting engaged. He'd literally said nothing of it.

She turned on the faucet, grateful for cold water to shock her back to her senses. She'd just dried her face when the back door opened and Sarena walked in. "See? There she is. I told you Auntie Sorrell would be back today."

Sorrell turned and met her eldest sister's eyes. She carried her three-month old baby on her hip and wore the widest smile Sorrell had ever seen. "He's so big," she said, rushing forward to take her nephew. "Hey, baby. Do you remember me?" Tears flowed down her face as Sarena passed West to her.

"What's wrong?" she demanded.

Sorrell pulled in a tight breath and shook her head. She

smiled at West, but it pulled so hard against her face, she thought it might break.

"Sorrell," Sarena said, plenty of warning in her voice.

"Theo broke up with me," she said, the words rushing out of her. She half-laughed at the chubby baby in her arms and half-sobbed as the truth came out.

"Oh, no," Sarena moaned, taking Sorrell into her arms. "Why? You guys were doing so good."

"I messed it up," Sorrell said into her sister's shoulder. West began to fuss, because he was smashed between the two of them, and Sarena took the baby back. She went into the living room and laid him on the floor before dragging a toy over and positioning it over him so he could reach up with his hands and feet and touch the brightly colored shapes.

She turned back to Sorrell, who made her way to the huge dining room table and sank into a chair. "I'm calling Seren."

"I don't care," Sorrell said, still weeping. "Tell her. Tell the world. It doesn't matter."

"You're going to get him back."

"I don't think so." Sorrell shook her head. "Not this time, Sarena. You didn't see him."

"Seren, I need you at the farmhouse right now...yes. Now. It's Sorrell." She hung up as she sat at the table too. "She's on her way. Five minutes."

Sorrell put her head down in her arms and let herself cry quietly. "I was doing so good, too, Sarena. I was. I haven't cried like this in months. I only got emotional a couple of times at the cabin. I've been so strong."

She didn't feel strong now. She felt like a complete waste of a human being, and she couldn't believe she'd hurt Theo again. "I didn't want to hurt him," she said, feeling reckless and out of her head. "Why did you let me hurt him? That's all I didn't want to do. I prayed so hard to not do that."

Sarena put her hand on Sorrell's back, and for a moment, Sorrell thought it was the touch of her mother. Hope filled her for a fraction of a second, and then the reality of her life shattered her soul all over again.

She hadn't calmed by the time Serendipity walked through the back door. Strode was a better word for it, and she wore her frustration and irritation plainly on her face. Sorrell met her eye, and everything about Serenidipity softened.

"You broke up with him," she said, stalling several paces away. She looked from Sarena to Sorrell. "Go fix it, Sorrell. Go right now. I don't care how far you have to go or what you have to say. But go fix it."

"I can't," she said. "And I didn't break-up with him. He broke up with me."

"What?" Serendipity looked from sister to sister. "That makes no sense. He's been in love with you for years."

"She's right," Sarena said.

Sorrell didn't need Serendipity's harsh tone right now. She needed someone to love her unconditionally.

Theo does.

She pushed the thought away, because it simply wasn't true.

Serendipity sighed and took a spot across the table from

Sorrell and Sarena. "Well?" she demanded. "What happened?"

Sorrell said nothing, because Sarena could relate the story as well as she could. She heaved a sigh and filled Serendipity in while Sorrell continued to weep.

"This is nothing," Serendipity said. "This is you getting in your car and going to find him, Sorrell. Right now." She stood up as if she'd be leaving with Sorrell. "I mean it."

"I can't," Sorrell said.

"I heard you say that for months," Serendipity said. "It's just a lie you tell yourself, because you're afraid." She leaned into the table. "Honestly, Sorrell, what were you thinking?'

"Seren," Sarena said. "This isn't what she needs."

"No, it is exactly what she needs," Serendipity said. "We've coddled her, Sarena. We've supported her. We've sat with her while she completely breaks down. We build her back up every dang time. She needs to get over her pride, and get to wherever Theo is, and make it right."

She made all of that sound so easy. Sorrell glared at her. "I am sobbing my eyes out. I have no pride left."

"Yes, you do," she said. "This started because you were upset about me and Sarena talking about you and Theo? Come on." She scoffed and walked into the kitchen. She filled a glass with water while Sorrell stared after her, her eyes wide.

"Honestly, what did you think your life with him would be like?" she asked, turning back to the pair of them. "Did you think he'd move into this old house with you? Live on a ranch that's not his? Honestly, Sorrell."

"I didn't think..." She let her voice trail off, because that was exactly right. She hadn't thought about it.

"Well, think about it," Serendipity said. "Then go find him, and tell him all your hopes and dreams for a future together with him." She practically slammed the glass down on the counter. "Because we are not doing this again." She looked from Sarena to Sorrell again. "Come on, Sarena. We're *not* doing this again." She headed for the back door as if she'd leave, and shock vibrated through Sorrell. Surely they wouldn't leave.

Sarena stood up and collected West from the living room. She cast Sorrell a mournful look as she went by, and she actually left the farmhouse first.

Serendipity held the door, her gaze sharp as she watched Sorrell from the doorway. "You love him, Sorrell. He loves you. I don't know what you need to do to make it right, but you better figure it out. Sarena and I will start praying that Theo has the forgiving heart we think he does."

With that, her younger sister walked out, and Sorrell was once again alone in the farmhouse.

Sorrell was so shocked she stopped crying. She drew in deep breath after deep breath, finally feeling her mind start to work from a place of calmness instead of panic.

Ideas flowed from one side of her brain to the other, and she got up to collect one of her notebooks from the office. Back at the dining room table, she started to list out her thoughts, getting them out of her head and onto something concrete she could look at and make sense of.

Half an hour later, she'd scribbled all over one page, and she circled the thing that mattered most to her.

It was Theo's name.

He mattered most to her.

She looked up and out the windows that stretched across the back wall of the farmhouse. How many times had he walked through that door to greet her? So many. She'd never known if he'd had a bad day or not, because he'd always had a smile for her. He was always so focused on making sure she was okay and that she was happy.

After studying the paper again, she could see action steps open up right in front of her.

She flipped the page and made a list quickly.

1. Quit my job
2. Find Theo
3. Apologize
4. Tell him I love him
5. Beg him for another chance
6. Ask him to take me to the wilds of the Hill Country, where we'll live down a dirt road with a big house at the end of it and a gate to mark our property
7. Marry Theo
8. Have a family with Theo
9. Grow old with Theo

She disliked that she didn't have ten things on her list, but she didn't waste another moment stewing over it. She was done doing that. She picked up her phone and acted, reaching down deep for the courage she'd need to have to make it to step six.

"Step six," she whispered as her boss's phone line rang. "Just make it to step six, and you'll be home free."

CHAPTER 21

Everything hurt, and Theo rolled his shoulders to try to get the zinging pain to stop. He hadn't done much physical labor around the cabin, as the garage had a snowblower he'd used to clear the driveway for him and Sorrell.

The most he'd done was carry in bags of groceries and walk the puppies down the cleared roads. Now, at Chestnut Ranch, he was lifting heavy bales of hay and straw, wrestling with cattle to get them to go into chutes they didn't want to go into, and fitting fences into holes that were far too small to hold them.

It had only been two days since he'd started at Chestnut Ranch, and there was not enough painkiller to calm his muscles and soothe his aching heart. He hadn't gone to town to get a new phone, and he thought maybe he simply wouldn't. It was nice not being chained to a device. He didn't have to look at his phone screen and get his heart ripped out over and over when he found it blank.

Sorrell had never called or texted after he'd left Fox Hollow the first time, and he had no reason to think she would this time. Leaving the phone behind in Amarillo was actually a blessing—unlike this stubborn cow that he couldn't get to cooperate with him.

"Come on," he muttered, and he finally got the final leg into the chute. The cow grumbled at him, but Theo didn't care. He had a dozen more to get into the chute so they could get their eyes checked, and then he could retreat to his silent cabin for something to eat. That afternoon, he had fields to attend to, as Seth had put him on a quarter of the agriculture here at the ranch.

Apparently, he'd been understaffed for the last few months, and the amount of work the ranch needed seemed never-ending. Theo didn't mind, because he didn't want to sit around his empty cowboy cabin and do nothing.

Then he'd just think about the mountain cabin, and Sorrell. Everything in his life led back to Sorrell, and Theo didn't know what to do about that. How did he move past her?

He herded another cow toward the chute, and thankfully, this one just did what he wanted and went inside. "You'll have to leave the state," he told himself. Perfect desperation and helplessness filled him.

He had nowhere to go. Nothing he wanted to do. No one he wanted to become.

He didn't want his own ranch, so working someone else's had been easy for him. He didn't want to wear suits and trade stocks, though he loved checking on his investments and taking risks with buying and selling. It was still a hobby, not a career.

He didn't *need* a career.

He loved Texas, and he loved wearing a cowboy hat. He didn't want to go back to Georgia or South Carolina. There were ranches all over Texas, and it was a huge state. The best he could hope for was that if he put enough distance between him and Chestnut Springs, he'd be able to recover from this disaster.

With all the cattle in the chute, he closed the gate behind the last one and turned around. Sweat ran down the side of his face, and he wiped it away.

"Lunch break," Rex Johnson said, and Theo returned the grin the other man had on his face.

"Thank goodness," Theo said. "It's hot today."

"And it doesn't help that these are the most stubborn herd of cattle we've had in years." Rex chuckled, and he turned as a child's voice filled the air.

He laughed as his daughter skipped up to him, and he scooped her into his arms. "Where's Mom?" he asked, glancing beyond the corral where Theo still stood. He had to get out of there, because he couldn't handle the sight of a happy family right now.

He ducked under the fence rung and came face-to-face with Holly, Rex's wife. She was easily six months pregnant, and she grinned at Theo. "Hello," she said.

"This is our new man," Rex said. "Theo Lange. My wife, Holly."

"Yes, I heard when you two got married," Theo said. The ranch community wasn't that big, especially in this area. While he hadn't been invited to the wedding, he'd heard the news. "I don't know your daughter's name, though." He grinned at the girl in Rex's arms.

"Sarah," Rex said. "If we have another girl, what are we going to name her? Huh?" He seemed so happy as he gazed at his daughter.

"Ivy," Sarah said.

"What if it's a boy?" Theo asked.

"Joseph," Sarah said. She was the cutest thing on the planet, and Theo's smile turned genuine.

"Did you guys bring me lunch?" Rex asked, stepping past Theo to take his wife's hand.

"It's at the homestead," Holly said as they turned away. "We better hurry, or Russ and Griffin will eat it all."

"Must be pizza, then," Rex said with a laugh.

Theo watched them go, an invisible barrier separating him from them. They existed on a completely different plane than he did, and the path to where they were was completely inaccessible to him.

His heart beat in his chest, but he honestly wasn't sure how. The mental anguish pressing on him overwhelmed him, and he reached out to steady himself against the fence beside him. "How do I do this?" he asked, looking up into the sky above.

It seemed made of nothing but emptiness, and Theo

hated it. He wanted to be back in Colorado, in that cabin, where he didn't have to worry about his next job, or if he'd run into Sorrell simply by going to buy milk.

He headed away from the corral and toward his cabin, which at least had air conditioning. He had milk already too, and he could order his groceries and have them delivered.

"No," he muttered to himself. "You're not going to do that, because you're not staying here." He'd run away from Sorrell before, and he wasn't too proud to do it again.

She'd told him at the cabin she didn't like it when he disappeared, but Theo was having a hard time believing anything that had happened at the cabin. It felt like another world, where the things that had been said and done there weren't real. Now that he and Sorrell were back to the real world, her true feelings had manifested themselves.

He wondered how long it would take to stop thinking about her. He'd been at The Singer Ranch for two months and hadn't achieved that. Six months? A year?

He wasn't sure he could survive that long with her in his head. She was so prevalent, when he looked up, he saw her sitting on the back steps of his cabin, all three puppies near her. She'd been in his house if the dogs were out...

Theo froze, the world spinning twice as fast now. Three times. So fast, Theo could barely hold on. His breath whiplashed through his lungs, and he realized he wasn't hallucinating when the form of Sorrell stood up and wiped her hands down the front of her shorts.

She took a couple of steps toward him before she stopped.

Theo didn't want to stand in the sun and have this conversation. He strode forward, though his legs felt like brittle sticks of spaghetti that might break at any moment. "You don't belong here, Sorrell," he said as he brushed by her.

"Theo," she said, but he would not be swayed by her voice. Not again.

"These are *my* dogs," he said over his shoulder. "You don't get to come take them when you want."

"I knocked," she said. "They started whining, that was all. I let them out to sit with me."

"Go home," Theo said as he started up the steps. Just a few more, and he'd be inside. He could shut her out and pretend she hadn't come to see him.

She came to see you!

The stupid thought brought hope with it, and Theo didn't want that.

"Theo, please," she said, her voice far too close for her to still be standing in the yard. Sure enough, when he entered the house and held the door for the dogs to come in, Sorrell was right there with them.

Her dark hair had been pulled back, leaving her pretty face unobscured. She hadn't been crying, and Theo wasn't sure if he was happy about that or not.

"I'm not leaving," she said, her voice strong. "I have to talk to you."

Theo retreated further into the house. "I get thirty minutes for lunch," he said. "If you have to talk, that's how long you get."

If she actually talked that long, Theo might lose his mind, but he couldn't take back the words. He busied himself in the kitchen, first getting the dogs fresh water and then opening his fridge to find something to eat. He hadn't cooked or ordered anything in the past two days, so his fridge didn't have a lot to offer.

He closed it and opened a cupboard to pull out a can of chili. He didn't want something hot on this abnormally warm winter day, and he hesitated. Why hadn't he thought about what he'd eat for lunch and dinner?

Probably because Sorrell took every brain cell he possessed, and eating didn't matter.

"I won't take your whole lunch," she said. "I am hopelessly in love with you. I don't know why you reacted so badly to what I said in the hotel, and it doesn't matter. I'm sorry I implied or made you think that a relationship with you is ridiculous. It isn't. It's all I want. All I've wanted for a long time."

Theo looked down at the counter, letting her words wash over him. He put both hands on the countertop and pressed, using the solid surface to ground himself.

"I'm sorry I said no so often," she said. "I'm sorry I didn't put your opinion above that of my sisters'. I'm sorry I didn't think as far down the road as I needed to." She paused for a moment, but Theo couldn't look at her quite yet.

"I've looked down that road, Theo," she said. "I can see us on a big piece of land somewhere, in a big, yellow house, with a long, dirt road driveway, with one of those gray-brick gates just off the highway. And there's this sign that says Lange Longhorns on one side, with a big, metal Texas star on the other, that I keep freshly painted because we're Texan, and we love being Texan." Her voice broke, but she continued anyway. "We go to the Colorado cabin every Christmas, and we take the kids and the dogs and we don't let anyone tell us how to celebrate Christmas. We eat fried chicken on Christmas Eve when everyone else is opening new pajamas and eating ham and drinking sweet tea."

Theo turned toward her, his pulse sounding in his ears as it throbbed through his whole body.

"I have your phone," she said, stepping forward and setting it on the counter between them. "You left it in the hotel." She cleared her throat. "I'm here, because I love you. I'm sorry for everything I've put between us, and kept between us. I am begging you to forgive me, and I'm going to beg for just one more chance. I will not put anything or anyone above you. You're all I want."

She started to dig in her pocket, but Theo didn't need her to say anything else. Before he could tell her that, she pulled out a piece of paper and unfolded it. "I made this list of what I wanted, and look, Theo, it's only you."

Sorrell held up the paper, and even from ten feet away, he could see his name in black letters, with several circles around it. The rest of the words were basically scribbles, and he could see her desperation and franticness in the writing.

"It's always been you," she said. "I want the house, and the gate, and the kids. I want it all, but none of it really matters if I can't have you."

She drew in a big breath and nodded. "Okay, that's all. That's the first six steps."

Theo cocked his head at her, unsure about what that meant. "What's step seven?" he asked.

Sorrell blinked, clearly surprised. Instead of answering vocally, she reached into her other pocket and took out another piece of paper. She put it next to the first one on the counter, and Theo took a couple of steps and picked it up.

1. Quit my job
2. Find Theo
3. Apologize
4. Tell him I love him
5. Beg him for another chance
6. Ask him to take me to the wilds of the Hill Country, were we'll live down a dirt road with a big house at the end of it and a gate to mark our property
7. Marry Theo
8. Have a family with Theo
9. Grow old with Theo

He read it quickly, that seedling of hope that had started when he'd entered his cabin growing rapidly.

He looked up at her, searching her expression, which held anxiousness and hope. She fiddled with the buffalo turquoise ring, which she now wore on her left ring finger.

Theo could float away on the hope filling him now.

"Is this a proposal?" he asked.

Sorrell opened her mouth, paused, and then said, "Yes."

"Yes?" Theo asked, glancing down at the paper again. *Grow old with Theo.* That sounded absolutely heavenly. "What if I want to ask you and hear a yes?"

Sorrell took a couple of steps forward. "What step are we on?" she asked.

"You quit your job," he said. "You found me. You've apologized, told me you loved me, begged for another chance, and asked me to take you to the wilds of the Hill Country." He looked up at her, his heartbeat sprinting. He lifted the paper. "You missed a step."

"I did?"

"There's sort of a leap between six and seven, don't you think?" He turned the paper toward her. "You do all of these things, and then bam, we're married."

"You think we need more time to date?" She looked from the paper to him, and their eyes locked.

Theo wanted to tease her that she hadn't left him room to accept her apology, tell her he loved her too, and allow him time to plan the perfect proposal. Instead, he reached for her, cradled her face in his hands, and leaned down to kiss her.

She pulled in a breath through her nose, tense in front of him. Then she melted into his touch, her hands coming up to push his cowboy hat off his head and through his hair.

"I love you," he whispered. "You forgot to put that on the list." He kissed her again, bringing her as close to him as he could.

His head cleared, and Theo could see everything

perfectly now. "I accept your apology," he said as he moved his mouth to her neck. "You forgot that too."

She sighed as she clung to his shoulders and pressed into his touch. "I can add them to the list."

"I want to ask *you* to marry *me*," he said next, pulling back and looking at her. "Because I need to hear you say yes, Sorrell."

"I'll say yes," she promised.

"Is there a timeframe we're talking about?" he asked. "Because I don't have a ring yet, sugar."

"Mm." She smiled up at him. "No timeframe."

Theo met her eyes. "Do you want to go shopping for the ring with me?" He wanted to walk off this ranch and get to a jewelry store right now.

"Yes," she said.

"We can start looking for that big piece of land too," he said. "If you're really willing to leave the farmhouse."

Sorrell reached up and slid her hand up the side of his face. Theo fell in love with her over and over as they looked at one another. "I will go anywhere to be with you."

Theo grinned, and he leaned down and kissed the woman he loved one more time.

CHAPTER 22

Sorrell peered out her window as Theo slowed down, the road he'd be turning on coming up on the right. "I don't like this fence," she said.

"Everything's changeable," he said, echoing something their realtor had said at the first property they'd visited.

"Mm hm," she said, eyeing the horrible rocks like they'd been put there purposely to annoy her. "Those don't look like they'll be coming down without a fight." There was so much cement between the rocks that Sorrell thought it was a fight that even Theo might lose.

He'd been working at Chestnut Ranch for the past three months. Sorrell had found a new job, and now she worked from home, doing online customer service for an airline. She liked that she could set her schedule from week to week, that the hours were flexible, and that she didn't have to attend long meetings and wear heels anymore.

She really was so much happier, and she hadn't even realized how unhappy she was until she'd removed herself from some situations.

She still didn't have a diamond ring on her left ring finger, but she and Theo had been to a couple of jewelers in the past month or so. This was their third weekend out in the Hill Country, and Sorrell was starting to feel bad for their realtor.

Theo made the turn, and once they were past the hideous gate, Sorrell took a deep breath. "It's nice back here."

"I think this will be the one you like the best," Theo said.

"I hate it when you do that," she said. "Let's just go into it fresh. No preconceived notions."

He just chuckled, because they'd had this talk before. He said they'd poured over the pictures online and chosen to drive out here to see the house and property, because they liked what they saw.

She said it was completely different to see things in real life. She couldn't tell how the rooms flowed together, or where they were placed, in pictures. She wanted to go in fresh, despite the fact that she had made a binder with notes on the properties they'd requested to see.

A blip of irritation moved through her, and now she didn't want to like this one at all just so he wouldn't be right. The fields lining the dirt lane were well-maintained, with intact fences and trees still standing where they'd been growing for years.

She liked that. She saw no reason to cut down trees if it wasn't necessary.

Once around a bend in the road, the house came into view, and Sorrell pulled in a breath and held it. It was yellow, and Sorrell was very aware that she'd seen these pictures before. She'd also said when she'd shown up at Theo's weeks ago that she wanted a big, yellow house for them to grow old in.

There it was.

"It's nice," Theo said.

"Out here," Sorrell said, because she didn't want to start liking this place yet. It was their third one today, and they had one more to get to. It was the tenth or eleventh property they'd taken a tour of, and Sorrell wondered if they'd ever find the perfect place for them.

Theo brought the truck to a stop and looked out through the windshield. "It's big."

"Yes, it is." Sorrell knew how big. She'd memorized the real estate listing. "Let's go."

"Amanda's not here yet."

"She's right behind us." Sorrell opened her door and slid from the truck, the April afternoon warm and muggy. She pushed her hair off her forehead, wishing she'd pulled it back.

"Nice lawn," Theo said, meeting her at the front of the truck. She slipped her hand into his, noticing the front porch that wrapped around the corner. The roof hung over the porch too, providing shade where she'd like to sit and read.

The yard was taken care of, as were the flowerbeds. The house had a detached two-car garage, and an attached two-car garage. A cement pad made a driveway where they could park and not be in the dirt or mud, and Sorrell liked that too.

Amanda didn't come rumbling down the road, and Sorrell's impatience grew. They didn't normally go inside a property without their realtor, because she had the codes to get through the lockboxes.

Today, though, Theo went right up the front steps to the door and tried turning the knob. Miraculously, the door opened, and Sorrell met his eye.

"It's okay, sugar," he said. "She really should be here any minute, and we had a scheduled showing. No one's here."

Sorrell ducked in front of him and entered the house. A grand staircase went up at the back of the foyer, with a hallway running alongside it to the back of the house. A doorway to her left led into an office, and Sorrell looked in there.

"I hate it when you're right," she said, looking over her shoulder to Theo.

He grinned at her. "You like this place, don't you?"

"I *hate* that gate."

Theo gathered her into his arms, and Sorrell eased right into his chest, his smile contagious enough to infect her. "Sweetheart, I have plenty of money to change that gate to anything you want."

"I want gray brick," she said. "With—"

"A sign that says Lange Longhorns on one side and a big, metal Texas star on the other," they said together.

Theo chuckled. "I know, baby. I was listening that day in my cabin."

"Do you really want longhorns?" she asked.

"Sure," he said. "I mostly want horses, though."

"This place is eleven acres," she said. "With horse barns and corrals. Plenty of room for that."

"Let's look at the kitchen," he said. "That's going to make or break it for you."

She'd seen the pictures, and she knew this house had an amazing chef's kitchen. It was one of her top pluses about the property. It had only been on the market for four days, and Sorrell had been excited when Amanda had sent it to them.

She went past the staircase, the hallway opening up to a large room that housed the living room, dining area, and kitchen. "Open concept," she said.

"I can see your family here," he said. "Seren on the couch with Brian and their dogs, while you're in the kitchen with me, and we're making bacon jam to go with the ham and cheese croissants."

Sorrell started laughing, because she'd just presented him with the menu she wanted to make for Serendipity's wedding. The big event was only one month away, and Sorrell needed to finalize the menu and start ordering the groceries she needed.

Theo went toward the kitchen, but she trailed her hand along the back of a large sectional couch, admiring the huge wall of windows with a set of French doors that led out onto the deck on this side of the house. She went that way and looked out the doors. "All covered over here too," she said. "Look, there's a playset."

She turned back and found Theo standing next to the island in the kitchen, an enormous vase of red roses beside him. Those hadn't been there before...

Sorrel took a couple of steps as she took in the sexy cowboy and the beautiful flowers. She stalled as he got down on both knees and held up a black box.

"Sorrell Adams," he said. "I've loved you for a long time. I want to be your husband, and I want you to be my wife. I want to have a family with you, and grow old with you, and I think we should do all of that right here, in this house. This is where our life together begins. Will you marry me?"

"Yes," Sorrell said, her voice strong and sure. "Yes, Theo. All day and all night, yes." She flew toward him, and Theo rose to receive her into his arms. She pressed a sloppy kiss to his mouth and said again, "Yes."

Theo laughed and tried kissing her again. He didn't quite hit his mark, but it didn't matter. He leaned his forehead against hers and said, "I came and looked at this house last night, sweetheart. It's the one. I already put in an offer."

Sorrell pulled away from him, her surprise only allowing her to say "What?"

"Don't be mad," he said. "I've looked at fifty properties with you online. I know what you like and what you don't. Amanda met me here last night, and we looked at the property. I knew you'd love it—minus the gate—and I didn't want to wait."

"What about the last one we're looking at today?" she asked.

"We're not." Theo shrugged. "Amanda's on her way back to Chestnut Springs, and we—" He stepped around her and opened the fridge. "Ah, yes. We are going to enjoy a feast." He removed something from the fridge and turned toward her.

He held an immaculately decorated chocolate cake, and Sorrell marveled at this man. He was so good, and so handsome, and so perfect for her. She couldn't believe she'd been so blind for so long, and she praised the Lord that her eyes had finally been opened.

"Cake for dinner?" she asked with a giggle.

"We'll call for fried chicken," he said, smiling as he set the cake next to the roses. "I've already checked, and almost every restaurant in San Marcos delivers to our address."

"You just have everything worked out, don't you?" she asked. She stepped over to the cake and swiped her finger through the frosting on the side of the cake. She put it in her mouth, the sweetness exactly what she needed.

"I try," Theo said, sweeping his arm around her waist. "I love you, Sorrell Adams."

"I love you, too, Theo Lange."

"Can we set a date now?" he asked. "Please?"

Sorrell pulled her phone from her back pocket and swiped to her calendar. "So we'll probably close here in thirty days or so, right?"

"Right."

"Serendipity's wedding is on May second," she said,

looking at the dates. "We'll close here on May seventh or eighth..." She looked up at him. "May ninth? Right here on this property?" She couldn't believe she'd even suggested such a thing. She'd dreamt of her wedding for years and years, but it suddenly didn't matter.

All she needed was a white dress, good food, and Theo in that cowboy hat. She could buy one tomorrow, order the second in ten minutes, and she knew Theo would show up.

"May ninth," he repeated. "I guess I can wait that long."

Sorrell loved that he wanted her as quickly as he could get her. She tapped on the date and typed in all capital letters MARRY THEO!

She turned toward him, pure joy filling her. "I love you so much. Thank you for being patient with me."

"Love you, sugar." He took her into his arms and kissed her again, and Sorrell lost herself to the touch and taste of him.

He pulled away too soon, and said, "Come on, sweetheart. I'll show you the rest of the house. You're really going to like the back garden."

* * *

Keep reading for the first 2 chapters of an exclusive series - the Chappell Brothers at the Blue Grass Ranch in Kentucky. **Winning the Cowboy Billionaire** is available in paperback!

SNEAK PEEK: WINNING THE COWBOY BILLIONAIRE, CHAPTER ONE

Olivia Hudson smoothed down the dress she wore, though it would never lay completely flat against her stomach. She carried about twenty-five extra pounds, and no matter how much she tried to lose the barrel around her waistline, it wouldn't go.

Perhaps she didn't try that hard. She did spend a lot of time on her feet, looking for new herbs, plants, and fruits to make into oils and fragrances for her handmade, deluxe perfumes. She distilled everything in her very own perfumery, and every bottle got a fancy gold and pink sticker that Olli had designed herself. She even peeled and stuck the stickers onto the bottles herself.

Virginia helped, of course. Olli's best friend helped with everything, including getting her this invitation to a wedding in Chestnut Springs, Texas.

Olli didn't know Theo Lange or Sorrell Adams, but Theo was Virginia's half-brother. Olli could still remember when Ginny had found out and how upset she'd been. To Olli's knowledge, Ginny hadn't spent much time with Theo at all; they never spoke; no attempt had been made to welcome him into the Winters family.

Olli knew how hard it was to break into the Winters inner circle, that was for sure. She'd been friends with Ginny for three years before she'd even been invited over to the sprawling mansion surrounded by huge barley, rye, wheat, and corn fields.

The Winters owned an old and reputable whiskey distillery in Kentucky, and Olli had a lot of respect for their family even if Ginny's father had been extremely difficult to deal with.

Theo was apparently one of his illegitimate children, and yet Ginny and her mother had chosen to attend his wedding. Olli threw a look to Wendy Winters, and the woman was poised and proper, as always.

Olli often wanted to be more like her, but she simply couldn't do it. She loved to laugh and she liked to drive around horse country with the top down on her old Mustang, breathing in the scent of fresh grass, pure sunshine, and the distinct scent of horses, hay, and dirt.

Today, though, there was no hay or dirt. Plenty of sunshine here in Texas in May, and lots of horses on this patch of land where they'd gathered for the wedding.

Ginny came into the room and scanned Olli. "You look beautiful." She linked her arm through Olli's with a smile. "Let's go sit down."

Ginny was the one with pure beauty radiating from her

high cheekbones, long limbs, and deep, nearly navy blue eyes. Olli giggled with her as they left the house and headed to the chairs that had been set up in the back garden.

The flowers and plants and grass bloomed earlier here in Texas than they did in Kentucky, and Olli's nose went into overdrive. "I want some of those flowers," she said, indicating a tall stalk with beautiful blooms protruding from each side of it every few inches. "Don't they smell amazing?"

"I thought you were working on masculine scents," Ginny said, steering Olli away from the flowers. She'd get a picture of them later, because she could then take them to her contact at the nursery, and he'd tell her what kind of flower they were.

"I am," Olli said. "I've got to break out of musk and pine." She glanced at a couple of cowboys who watched her and Ginny pass. She smiled at them, but she wasn't looking for a long-distance relationship. Olli wasn't looking for a relationship at all, unless one with a new investor for her perfumery counted.

She'd written and submitted four grants this year alone, and the waiting process could test even the most patient man. Heck, the Dalai Lama would probably find the process exhausting.

She sat, though, and she enjoyed the fans that blew from above in an attempt to keep the guests cool. Ginny's mother joined them, and a few moments later, the ceremony started to come together.

Theo, a tall, dark cowboy Olli might have found attractive once-upon-a-time took his place at the altar, a wide, hopeful smile on his face.

She'd felt like that once. Hopeful and happy about her romantic prospects. She'd dated plenty of men in her twenties and thirties. She'd even worn a diamond ring once.

She'd vowed she never would again, though. Not after she'd made it all the way through all the wedding preparations, the engagement pictures, the save-the-dates, the food sampling, and the formal pictures in the fields that surrounded her family farm.

She hadn't quite been stood up at the altar, but almost. Her fiancé had called the morning before the wedding, mere hours before the final rehearsal dinner. She'd invited her whole family to that. His too.

I can't do this, he'd said. *It has nothing to do with you, Olli. I swear.*

She almost scoffed right out loud at this wedding, five years later. She'd been in enough relationships to know that when one ended, it had something to do with her, even if her contribution was small.

She put her ex out of her mind as the wedding march started to play. Olli stood with the rest of the crowd, and she turned to watch the most beautiful woman walk down the aisle, one slow step at a time. She wasn't hanging on the arm of her father, obviously, as the man escorting her appeared to be about her same age.

Olli's curiosity lifted, as she loved getting to know people and learning their stories. Did she speak to her father?

Was he alive? Too sick to walk her down the aisle? What was the story there?

Olli loved stories, and the more personal, the better. She could take those ideas and transform them into scents for her perfumes and candles, and she'd always found the best inspiration from real life.

She sighed as the bride moved past her, and she enjoyed watching Theo and Sorrell get married right there in their own back garden. She'd been resistant to coming to this wedding with Ginny, but Ginny had pulled the best friend card, and Olli had been helpless at that point.

She'd bought a new dress, packed a bag, and come to Texas, a state she'd never visited before.

"Sorrell," Theo said. "I've loved you for seven long years. Eight maybe." He ducked his head, and Olli sighed again, this time pressing her hand over her pulse. She'd always had a weakness for soft-yet-tough cowboys, and Theo seemed like exactly that type.

"I promise to love you and take care of you for the rest of my life." He looked up at her, the joy on his face something Olli wished she could bottle and sell.

Radiant joy, she thought. *Smells like sunshine, weddings, and...* She cast a look to that flower, thinking it would be perfect for her bright yellow Radiant Joy candle. The one she hadn't developed yet.

"Theo," Sorrell said. "You've shown more patience than any man I've ever met. I love you, and I'm grateful for you. I know we'll have an amazing life together, no matter what comes our way."

Olli couldn't help smiling as the pastor pronounced them man and wife, and Theo leaned down to kiss his new wife. She'd been to plenty of weddings in Kentucky, with plenty of cowboys, but the whooping and heehawing that erupted from this group was enough to startle her pulse into overdrive.

"My goodness," she said, looking at Ginny. They burst out laughing together, and Ginny leaned toward her.

She had to practically yell, "Texas cowboys are different than Kentucky cowboys, I guess," for Olli to hear her.

Olli looked around, thinking that they might be louder, but to her, the cowboys here looked and smelled and acted a lot like the ones she knew back home.

She was fine being friends with them. She just didn't want one coming into her life and trying to take over her business—or her heart—again.

"What do you mean?" she asked a few days later. "The grant didn't say anything about being married."

"You don't need to be married, Miss Hudson," the man on the other end of the line said, his tone somewhat rounded and clipped at the same time. He definitely wasn't from the South, and Olli wished her accent wasn't quite so thick. "Mister Renlund simply wants to make sure his investment is going to a family company."

Olli didn't know what to say. She'd missed that requirement in the grant application.

"He very much likes your proposal," Benjamin said, continuing despite the tailspin Olli's thoughts had gone into. "He found it so different from what we usually get. You're on the list of his top five, and he comes around and visits everyone and their businesses before he decides on the grant money."

"You're kidding," Olli said, looking around. Her perfumery sat in a state of chaos at the moment, with vials and bottles all over the place. She'd learned the flower in Texas was called a gladiolus, and she'd already ordered several varieties to be delivered in the next week or so.

"I am not kidding, Miss Hudson," Benjamin said. "We're looking at being there in about two weeks. Does that work for you?"

Olli reached for her desk calendar, clearing away a couple of pieces of unopened mail, a pile of rubber bands, and one of unmade boxes for her sample bottles of perfumes. "Uh, two weeks?" That would put them in the third week of May. "How long will Mister Renlund want to be here?"

Would she have to house him? Show him around Lexington? Her mind raced with the possibilities, and she reminded herself that she was very personable. She'd worked as a tour guide on two horse farms in the area before achieving her dream of opening and operating her own perfumery.

"Only a few days, ma'am. I'll send you his itinerary. He'd love to meet your husband or boyfriend."

Olli sat back, her frustration morphing into anger. "What if I don't have a husband or boyfriend?"

"That's why I call in advance," Benjamin said. "If I were you, Miss Hudson, I'd get one, even for a few days. In two weeks' time."

She opened her mouth to respond, but she blanked.

"Good day," Benjamin said, and the call ended. Olli scoffed as she took the phone from her ear and checked to make sure he'd hung up.

"Unbelievable," she muttered to herself. "That guy lives in the eighteen hundreds." Didn't he know women could—and did—run their own businesses these days?

No man needed.

Olli stared out the window across the room from her desk, trying to think of a single man she could somehow convince to be her boyfriend for a few days.

She'd grown up here in the Lexington area, and she knew a lot of people, but the only men who came to her mind were the Chappell brothers.

They owned Bluegrass Ranch, which happened to be located right next door to Olli's place. She saw at least five of them ride by her window on any given day of the week.

She stood up and went to the window, looking left and right as if one of them would happen upon her and offer her a diamond ring. One didn't.

Her stomach writhed, but no one else had called about any of the other grants. Two of them had rejected her on the same day yesterday, in fact.

Desperation clogged in her throat, and it wasn't pleasant. She squared her shoulders and started for the door. She could go next door and see what was happening with the

Chappells. In the back of her mind, she thought she'd heard that a couple of them had started dating someone recently.

But there were eight to choose from. It couldn't be that hard to get one of the boys next door to be her arm candy for a few days.

Olli stopped by the door of her perfumery and picked up a bottle of her newest scent, Seduction.

"Perfect," she muttered, spritzing the perfume on her neck and mostly bare shoulders. "Game on, boys."

She left the perfumery and looked to the road that ran east and west in front of her workshop. Her windows faced south, and she'd seen someone go by about a half an hour ago.

"What are you going to do? Stand on the side of the road and flag him down?" She didn't even know who she'd get next.

She decided it didn't matter, as long as it was one of the older Chappell brothers. She was forty-four, and she knew Cayden Chappell was her same age.

"No problem," she said. She didn't have Cayden's number, but she had Spur's. He was the oldest brother, and they'd exchanged numbers years ago when she'd first moved in next door.

"Just in case," he'd said.

Olli hadn't known what that had meant at the time, but she did now. Just in case his cattle got out. Just in case his horses broke through a fence. Just in case the Chappells had to turn off the water to the whole street—which was just their place and hers—for some ranch construction. Just in case he had to tell her the big rigs would be coming to get the horses they'd sold. Just in case he needed the field she owned between their places for all of his high rollers to park.

There had been a lot of instances of *just in case* over the years with Spur Chappell.

She'd spoken to Spur on all of those occasions. Spur rarely wore a smile, and though she'd known him for years, he still intimidated her.

So definitely Cayden, she told herself, still standing on her front porch. Foolishness rushed through her, and she couldn't get herself to take a single step.

A loud whistle rent the country silence, and Olli whipped her attention to the left, toward the sound.

She became aware of dogs barking, and the thundering of horses hooves, and another earsplitting whistle. "Ho, there," a man yelled, and Olli watched as Spur Chappell rode right in front of her on a magnificent bay horse.

She fell backward at the sudden appearance of him, realizing that he'd put himself between her and an oncoming herd of sheep.

A scream came from her mouth as she steadied herself against the door, and then Spur rode in front of her again, yipping and yelling at someone or something else. The dogs kept barking and barking, and just like someone had put up an invisible fence, the swarm of sheep turned away from her and her house and went in a wide arc toward the south.

Olli pressed her palm over her heartbeat, watching the fifty or so sheep flow away from her.

The dogs went with them, but Spur himself turned and

looked at Olli, their eyes meeting and locking for what felt like forever.

A grin danced across his face, and he lifted one gloved hand and acknowledged her before pressing his cowboy hat further onto his head and galloping after the sheep.

"Oh, my..." Olli let her words hang there, all of her focus now on the handsome cowboy who would look *mighty* fine on her arm for just one night.

Sneak Peek: Winning the Cowboy Billionaire, Chapter Two

S pur Chappell hated sheep with everything in him. They had a special talent for getting out of their fences, though they literally had the smallest brains of all farm animals.

He hated that they even had sheep at Bluegrass Ranch, but his youngest brother had insisted he get them. Spur had wanted to keep Duke on at the ranch, and he'd given in.

He wished now that he'd listened to his intuition, which had told him these sheep would be more trouble than they were worth. Not only that, but that Duke would not be around to tend to them properly.

He was off in Alabama this week, looking at two new mares he wanted to bring to the ranch, and that meant Spur was the one in the saddle with all the cattle dogs, trying to round up the naughty sheep.

Things happened swiftly from time to time, and he hadn't had a spare second to call or text Olivia Hudson, his next-door neighbor, and warn her about the sheep. There were only five dozen or so, but sheep could cause some damage if they were left unchecked.

Of course, they'd headed straight for her place the moment he'd swung into the saddle. Double of course, she'd been standing outside, waiting to be trampled by sheep.

He knew they wouldn't do that, but he'd still put himself and his dogs between the herd and the woman, because the last thing he and Bluegrass Ranch needed was a lawsuit.

Twenty minutes later, he had all the sheep back in their corral, where Blaine had fixed the fences they'd broken through. He touched his hand to his hat for his brother and called, "I have to go talk to Olli. They gave her a fright."

Blaine waved to indicate he'd heard Spur, and Spur set his sights on his one and only neighbor out here in the hills beyond Lexington. He loved the land out here, which always seemed to be made of emerald green grass and bright white fences. He loved the sky when it was pure blue, and when it had puffy clouds in it, and when the wind blew in a storm.

He loved the smell of fresh water in the stream on his land, and the scent of sawdust in the air from the new bridges he'd just put in.

His horse breathed rapidly, and Spur leaned down to pat All Out's neck. "Good boy," he said to the horse, the way one would to a dog. "We got 'em, thanks to you."

It was the dogs who'd really done most of the herding work, but Spur never told the horses that. His horses all believed they were kings and queens, because he raised them to be. They had championship blood in their veins, and he expected them to train and run like it.

That was how he made his money, after all. If he had a horse who wasn't a diva and couldn't run, he couldn't do anything with that horse. His family ranch depended on breeding and selling top-quality horses that would run until they day the dropped dead.

Not that Spur ever pushed them that far. But he had seen over a dozen of the horses he'd bred and sold win the Belmont, the Kentucky Derby, or the Preakness. Two of his horses had won all three in the same year, taking that Triple Crown.

Every time one of his horses won, any horse in that bloodline got more valuable. Spur kept immaculate records of the horse races around the world, and when he walked into an auction, everyone took note.

The woman next door didn't care about any of that, though, and Spur brought his ego back down to Earth as he went up the road to her house. He found her outside still, down on her hands and knees as she ripped up the flowers his sheep had trampled.

She heard him coming, and she got to her feet and wiped her sunkissed hair off her forehead. She cocked one hip while he brought All Out to a stop and swung out of the saddle.

"Hey, Olli," he said, walking toward her so he could see the damage in her flower garden.

"Spur," she said, clearly not happy with him.

"Sorry about the sheep." They'd done a number on

whatever she'd had growing there. "Tell me how much to fix that."

"You can't fix that," she said. "Those were my gardenias and a new crop of four o'clocks. I use that gardenia for my Down Home South candle." She glared at him.

"I'm sorry," he said, and he meant it. "Animals are unpredictable."

She took a step toward him, and he wouldn't have predicted she'd do that. His heartbeat skipped over itself for a moment, and he wasn't even sure why. He'd talked to Olli lots of times; she was pretty in a Southern belle kind of way, though he'd never let himself think about her for too long.

He hadn't let himself entertain thoughts about a woman for years now, though if he had, he could easily see himself fantasizing about the curvy, gorgeous Olivia Hudson.

She was still prowling toward him, something sparking in her eyes that interested him. Maybe he had thought a lot about Olli and had just never admitted it to himself. He pushed against the idea now too.

"I can pay for the damage," he said, clearing his throat as her perfume hit his nose. She smelled amazing, like lemons and vanilla and cookies. He wanted a taste of her right then, and he couldn't believe himself.

"I can have one of my men come replant the flowers," he said, sticking to facts to keep his brain in control of this situation. "I know they won't be good enough or ready when you need them, but I'm not sure what else to do to make it right."

Olli stopped a couple of feet from him and looked him

up and down. Spur suddenly wished he wasn't sweaty and dusty from rounding up the sheep. He held his ground, glad when her eyes finally returned to his.

"Sorry, Olli," he said again, wishing she'd name her price so he could go.

"You can do all of that," she said. "And I need one more favor, Spur."

"Name it," he said. "Along with the monetary amount, Olli."

"It'll be hundreds to pull out the ruined plants and put them in again." She switched her gaze to the flower garden, which was huge. Just how big Spur hadn't realized. He reminded himself that she ran a perfumery, and she grew most of the stuff she used to produce the fragrances herself.

"Include your lost product," he said. "I want to pay for that too."

"You will," she said. "I'll have to do some estimates."

"You have my number." He started to turn away from her magnetic gaze, telling himself not to ask her out right now. He couldn't even believe he was *thinking* about asking her out. His mother would be thrilled he was "getting back on the horse" again, but Spur wasn't.

He wasn't interested in dating. He *wasn't*. He simply couldn't admit his interest in Olli to himself. He first needed to figure out how long he'd be interested in her.

"Spur," she said, her voice even and calm.

"Hmm?" He looked back at her, unable to just walk away. Not while she wore that pale blue tank top and those denim shorts. Her hair fell in soft waves over her shoulders, and Spur just wanted to brush it back so he could feel her skin there, breathe in the scent of her, and kiss her.

He struggled to get control of his thoughts as she started speaking.

"Probably a thousand for the plants. Send over your guys to get this cleaned up and replanted." She cocked her head. "I'll text you about the lost product."

He nodded, something anchoring him in place. Maybe he didn't want to leave yet, but he couldn't fathom why he'd need to stay.

"The favor is that I need you to be my boyfriend for a few days," Olli said, holding his gaze with strength in her shoulders and back.

Spur stared at her, the words she'd said swimming through his whole system. He started laughing, because she couldn't be serious.

She smiled too, and Spur relaxed. She was just teasing him, something she'd done before when one of his studs had gotten out and kicked a hole through her storage shed. Then, she'd said she'd like to hire *him* out for a stud fee, and they'd had a good laugh together.

Today, though, she didn't join him, and he cut his laughter off pretty quickly. "I'll see who I have available to come do this," he said. "Could be a day or two."

"The party is in a couple of weeks," she said. "Might not even be a party. But you'll need to look nice, and wear that cowboy hat that you wear to church, and a pair of boots that you haven't worn on the ranch." She dropped her eyes to his current pair of cowboy boots, and Spur's pulse kicked at his ribs now.

"Party?" he practically growled.

"I have an investor interested in funding my business," she said, a slight frown appearing between her eyes. "He's very...traditional, and I've been told I need a husband or a boyfriend. A serious boyfriend." Those perfectly sculpted eyebrows went up, as if to ask him *Do you catch my drift, Spur?*

He caught it. He wasn't sure if he wanted to fist it tight and hold it close or throw it right back in her face.

"Dear Lord, you're not kidding," he said.

"I am not," she said, taking another step toward him. "It'll be for a few days at the most, Spur. It's a lot of money, and I need it."

His first instinct was to tell her he'd give her whatever money she needed. He had plenty of money, and not much time or patience for parties or small talk. Cayden, his next youngest brother was the public relations director for the horse breeding ranch. He was the one who cleaned up nice and entertained their buyers and sellers.

Spur had never cleaned his boots for a girlfriend, real or fake.

What if she wasn't fake? he thought, and he had no idea where that had come from.

"Okay," he said, just as surprised as Olli. He managed to keep his eyebrows down while hers went up again.

"Really?" she asked.

"It's a few days, right?" he asked. "I just ruined a lot

more work than that. I can wear a clean pair of boots and a nice hat for a few days."

"You'd just hang on my arm," she said with a smile. "Charm the socks off of the investor. It'll be easy."

Spur had never hung on anyone's arm, nor did he have much charm, so he didn't think it would be that easy, but he refrained from rolling his eyes. "Just tell me when," he said, taking the steps away from her that he needed to clear his head.

"I'll text you," she said, and Spur got himself back in the saddle, waved, and went back to Bluegrass Ranch.

Along the way, All Out nickered, as if asking Spur what in the world he'd been thinking.

"I don't know," he muttered as he arrived at the row house and started unsaddling the horse. What he did know was that Olli hadn't left his mind in the past twenty minutes, and that he couldn't get the tantalizing scent of her out of his nose.

He hadn't even known he had a crush on the woman, but his heart was testifying differently. Surprise accompanied Spur as he took care of his horse and put away the equipment he'd used.

He hadn't thought he'd ever want another girlfriend in his life, not after the break-up of his first marriage. He'd been stuck on Sydney for a long time after the divorce was final, and he'd never started dating again, though he probably could have five years ago.

"I never saw the point," he said to All Out as he gave the horse a bag of oats. "Is there a point to this?"

All Out snickered at him again, and Spur grinned at the horse. "No candy, boy. All we did was ride after some sheep." He stroked the horse's neck as he thought about Olli.

"I can't believe we can trick an investor if we don't get together beforehand," he said to the horse, seizing onto his own words. He pulled out his phone and called Olli, always preferring to just talk rather than text.

"Spur," she said, clear surprise in his voice.

"Heya, Olli," he drawled. "I was just thinking...this investor is probably pretty savvy. What's your plan for convincing him that we're a real couple?"

She didn't respond, and that was all the answer Spur needed. A smile touched his mouth again. "So do you want to go to dinner tonight? I feel like maybe we should get some facts in line before we have to convince anyone we're together."

"Facts?" she asked.

"Yeah," he said. "Wouldn't your boyfriend know a bit about your business? And maybe your middle name? Facts."

"Dinner tonight," she mused.

"I'm free every night this week," he said, wishing he could recall the words the moment he said them. He pressed his eyes closed, wondering if he'd just given away too much of what he was really feeling. As he waited for her to answer, he finally admitted to himself that he'd noticed Olli's pretty hair and quick smile years ago. He'd just shoved the feelings away whenever they came, and maybe now he wouldn't.

"I can go to dinner tonight," she said.

"I'll wear the hat and boots," he said. "You can check me off piece by piece."

She laughed, and said, "Okay, Spur. Seven?"

"See you at seven," he said. The call ended, and Spur just stood there, staring down the row of stalls where he kept his champions. "Who knew asking a woman out would be so easy?"

"Who'd you ask out?" Blaine asked, coming up behind Spur. "Momma's gonna freak out."

Spur flinched, because Blaine wasn't wrong. "It's nothing," he said. "Who have we got to send over to Olli's to fix her flower garden?"

Blaine sighed and shrugged. "I don't know. We're swamped over here, Spur."

They were, and Spur knew it. He put a growl on his face and in his voice when he said, "Fine, I'll do it," but he couldn't quite get himself to be unhappy about being able to go next door to see the woman again.

Dealing with his mother would be another issue, and Spur really *wasn't* looking forward to that. Thankfully, he only saw her on Sundays, and he still had five days before he'd have to face her.

Plenty of time to figure out if something with Olli could be real or if he'd just pretend to be her boyfriend so she could get the funding she needed. Then he could go back to pretending he hadn't thought about her in a romantic way.

You're such a liar, he told himself, but if Olli wasn't truly interested in him, Spur wouldn't open his heart for her to put new gashes on.

He knew better than that.

Winning the Cowboy Billionaire is available in paperback! **Will Olli be able to win over the cowboy billionaire? Or will she lose everything--including her heart?**

Chestnut Ranch Romance

Book 1: A Cowboy and his Neighbor: Best friends and neighbors shouldn't share a kiss...

Book 2: A Cowboy and his Mistletoe Kiss: He wasn't supposed to kiss her. Can Travis and Millie find a way to turn their mistletoe kiss into true love?

Book 3: A Cowboy and his Christmas Crush: Can a Christmas crush and their mutual love of rescuing dogs bring them back together?

Book 4: A Cowboy and his Daughter: They were married for a few months. She lost their baby...or so he thought.

Book 5: A Cowboy and his Boss: She's his boss. He's had a crush on her for a couple of summers now. Can Toni and Griffin mix business and pleasure while making sure the teens they're in charge of stay in line?

Book 6: A Cowboy and his Fake Marriage: She needs a husband to keep her ranch...can she convince the cowboy next-door to marry her?

Book 7: A Cowboy and his Secret Kiss: He likes the pretty adventure guide next door, but she wants to keep their relationship off the grid. Can he kiss her in secret and keep his heart intact?

Book 8: A Cowboy and his Skipped Christmas: He's been in love with her forever. She's told him no more times than either of them can count. Can Theo and Sorrell find their way through past pain to a happy future together?

BLUEGRASS RANCH ROMANCE

Book 1: Winning the Cowboy Billionaire: She'll do anything to secure the funding she needs to take her perfumery to the next level...even date the boy next door.

Book 2: Roping the Cowboy Billionaire: She'll do anything to show her ex she's not still hung up on him...even date her best friend.

Book 3: Training the Cowboy Billionaire: She'll do anything to save her ranch...even marry a cowboy just so they can enter a race together.

Book 4: Parading the Cowboy Billionaire: She'll do anything to spite her mother and find her own happiness...even keep her cowboy billionaire boyfriend a secret.

Book 5: Promoting the Cowboy Billionaire: She'll do anything to keep her job...even date a client to stay on her boss's good side.

Book 6: Acquiring the Cowboy Billionaire: She'll do anything to keep her father's stud farm in the family...even marry the maddening cowboy billionaire she's never gotten along with.

Book 7: Saving the Cowboy Billionaire: She'll do anything to prove to her friends that she's over her ex...even date the cowboy she once went with in high school.

Book 8: Convincing the Cowboy Billionaire: She'll do anything to keep her dignity...even convincing the saltiest cowboy billionaire at the ranch to be her boyfriend.

Texas Longhorn Ranch Romance

Book 1: Loving Her Cowboy Best Friend: She's a city girl returning to her hometown. He's a country boy through and through. When these two former best friends (and ex-lovers) start working together, romantic sparks fly that could ignite a wildfire... Will Regina and Blake get burned or can they tame the flames into true love?

Book 2: Kissing Her Cowboy Boss: She's a veterinarian with a secret past. He's her new boss. When Todd hires Laura, it's because she's willing to live on-site and work full-time for the ranch. But when their feelings turn personal, will Laura put up walls between them to keep them apart?

About Emmy

Emmy is a Midwest mom who loves dogs, cowboys, and Texas. She's been writing for years and loves weaving stories of love, hope, and second chances. Learn more about her and her books at www.emmyeugene.com.

Printed in Great Britain
by Amazon